RUN

Whisper Cove, Book 1

ALLISON LAFLEUR
BENEVA CLARK

Chapter One

Paige

Thump, swish.
Thump, swish.

The wipers' rhythmic sweeping helped calm my nerves, as I drove through the lightless night. The road got steeper and steeper, and the night darker and darker as the miles rolled by beneath the old pickup's worn tires. Its engine shuddered and wheezed, and the heater struggled in vain against the chill autumn air seeping through tiny gaps between the doors and windows. The cloudy headlights barely illuminated the asphalt ribbon ahead.

My skin crawled like a million ants raced just under my skin. Fine hairs on the back of my neck stood straight up. Like a nervous tick, I kept glancing in the rearview mirror, expecting to see headlights even though I had been alone on this road for the last hour. I leaned forward, trying to read an unlit sign along the road, hoping it would tell me where I was. My dry eyes blinked rapidly as blackness crept into the edges of my vision and fatigue threatened to drag me under.

After 36 straight hours behind the wheel, I *had* to be close.

Slowing down, I'd almost made sense of the reflective letters on the sign when suddenly all hell broke loose. Hooves and fur bounced over the hood and crashed against the windshield, which exploded in an intricate spider web crack. Suddenly blinded, I slammed on the brakes and held my breath as the truck fishtailed on squealing tires for what seemed like a slow eternity before veering off the slick road.

"Oh my God!"

Glass and blood rained down on me, and a moment later, I was falling, flipping downward. My head slammed against the steel door first and then the steering wheel. When the nightmare finally stopped, I was upside down with only the old seatbelt holding me in the cab as the truck hung suspended. Golden silence engulfed me for just a moment, but then the world erupted in a deafening song of bending steel and breaking glass. Pain wrapped itself around me before the darkness took me under.

Thump, swish.

Thump, swish.

Josh

"That's it, sweetheart. Just one more."

With one hand underneath the tiny body, I helped guide the pup out of Daisy as she struggled to deliver number seven—the runt of the litter. The newborn lay still, a golden mass barely covering the palm of my hand. I wiped the mucus from its mouth and nose and briskly rubbed its still chest, drying its fur and praying the pup was still with us.

"Is it?" Mack leaned over my shoulder, worry clouding his eyes as he watched the little one struggle to draw breath. Mama Daisy panted quietly in the straw.

"I'm trying, Mack." I hated the thought of losing it just as much as he did. This would probably be Daisy's last litter. At almost seven years old, the golden was nearing her senior years, which would be a loss for the whole town. Her pups were always in high demand.

I'd rubbed his fur dry, but the little guy still wasn't moving. Desperate to revive him, I leaned over the body cupped in my hands, and placed my mouth over his snout. With great care, I breathed a tiny puff, just enough of a whiff to inflate his dime sized lungs. Then I rocked back on my heels with the pup cradled in my hands, wiped a flannel sleeve across the sweat and dirt on my face, and watched for even a hint of improvement. Mack watched with me, both of us forgetting to breathe. Then the miracle happened.

A back leg jerked once. Twice. The puppy stretched, and his mouth opened with a tiny mewl. Unable to contain our enthusiasm, Mack and I cheered. We watched the clear signs of life with wide grins, and then I settled the pup in between his six suckling brothers and sisters, nose pointed at a teat. He latched on immediately, instinct unhindered by his brush with death.

Daisy craned her neck to look at her new litter as I cleaned her up, settling the new family into a big box with clean towels, close but not too close to the kerosene heater.

"Are they?" Mack asked, worry clinging to relief.

"They're all good. Mama and her babies are gonna be fine. Just keep an eye on that runt. Make sure they share, and he gets enough to eat."

"Thank you, Doc. Ma's got some chili on the stove. You hungry? It'll fill you up and keep you warm for the trek home. It's a miserable night to be driving through the woods."

"Thank you, Mack. That would be great. I've got an empty fridge at home. I don't think there's anything more than an egg and some pickles."

"Doc, you gotta get yourself a keeper. Marrying that woman in there was the best thing I ever did." He jutted his chin toward the house.

“No time for that right now. Anyway, I’ve got Chloe to help me take care of myself… if she ever comes back to work.” I smiled as I tried to wipe as much of the filth off me as I could. “I don't think even Chloe and the washing machine would save this shirt.”

Mack looked me over and shook his head. “Sorry about your shirt, Josh… and your jeans.”

“Good thing I buy them by the dozen. Nothing beats denim for durability. Just not great for attracting female attention.”

“Or maybe it’s the hours and that barnyard smell that follows you around.” He patted me on the back. "Come on, Doc. Let's go eat."

I sniffed myself and shrugged. "Lead the way, Mack.” *I'm not gonna get much sleep tonight, anyway.*

~

“Keep it together, Josh. Just a little longer.” I talked to myself to stay alert. It didn’t work. The asphalt blurred, merging with the woods. *Why don’t I get a place closer to town?*

Switching my foot to the brake, I slowed to a stop and shook my head to clear the cobwebs. I rolled the window down and let the cool night air wash over me. My eyes squeezed shut before I turned to the right and took the shortcut to town, too exhausted to make it all the way home. The emergency cot in my office would have to do. As tired as I was, I wouldn’t notice my feet hanging six inches off the end.

I rubbed my hand over my face as I drove. The-24-hour scruff scratched against my calloused hand. *Better get used to it. There’s no way you’ll have time to shave today.*

Mrs. Preston would be banging on the clinic door five minutes before opening, bringing her evil Pomeranian devil dog Muffy in for a teeth cleaning. The owner needed as careful handling as the patient. Mrs. Preston didn't like to be kept waiting. She believed early was on time, and in a town too small to keep a groomer, a vet would do. If it wasn't a teeth cleaning, she'd come in to get Muffy's nails cut. If it wasn't nails, it was weeping eyes. I knew she was just bored, but Muffy was the nastiest, yappiest creature that ever lived. I dreaded it, but at least for a teeth cleaning, I could knock her out with some anesthesia. The dog, I mean. Thank God for small miracles.

My exhausted mind mulled over the drudgery of the coming day, as I navigated the steep climb right before the sharp turn onto Shipwreck Road. If I hadn't known where I was going, I would have missed it entirely. Whisper Cove wasn't exactly the center of anything, and even the main route in and out of town was only an unlit one-lane expanse of pavement. With a population under 800 spread far and wide around a long-dead quarry, our stretch of Maine coast was home to more pets and livestock than people. Not exactly a hotbed of urban development, most roads didn't even have signs. We all found our way by memory. You could call it sleepy, but I preferred the term "peaceful."

Screeeeeeeeech!

I hit the brakes, and the truck's back end swung behind me in a violent fishtail before coming to rest next to a break in the steel guardrail. My fresh winter tires left the blacktop marred with swerving skid marks amongst the wreckage of whatever vehicle had gone through the rail and over the side. *Dammit. This is recent. They might still be down there.*

"Shit!" I glared at the destruction. All I wanted was to put my head on a soft pillow and close my eyes. Exhaustion coursed through every inch of me. Looking at the extent of the damage to the road, I knew responding would mean more hours before I got any sleep—*if* I got any sleep. Still, I was the closest thing to a doctor any crash victims were going to get for a long time, so I took a deep breath in through my nose, pushed open the door, and slid out.

Pain shot up from the soles of my aching feet as I stepped out onto the pavement and took in the scene of the accident. There was blood on the road and a broken antler lying on the shoulder. I expected to see a dead or injured deer, but the buck must have managed to walk away. The mangled chrome and broken glass told me the driver hadn't been so lucky.

Leaning over the shredded guard rail, I took a breath and forced myself to look down. Twenty feet below the road, precariously suspended in the trees, an old pickup sat mangled almost beyond recognition. Broken branches cradled the dented metal and camouflaged whoever was trapped inside.

I looked up and down the road, hoping in vain that one of Logan's deputies would show up right about now, but life doesn't work that way. With a sigh, I went back to my truck and dug a flashlight from where it had rolled under my seat. With a few knocks against the palm of my hand, the feeble light came to life. *You always forget to change the damn batteries.*

I grabbed my calf pulling rope from the truck and tied one end to an unbroken piece of guard rail and the other end around my waist before lowering myself like a rock climber down the steep slope until I was even with the wrecked vehicle.

The old truck hung nose down, suspended in the branches of two interlocked oak trees. Their trunks leaned under the pickup's weight as the branches cracked in the quiet night, letting the truck dip lower and lower. I could see a figure in the front seat, but fog clung to the cracked glass from the inside, making it impossible to see what or who I was dealing with.

"Hey!" I swung closer to the truck in an effort to grab the door, but I found it just out of my reach. "Are you okay?!" I swung back like a broken pendulum, but the figure in the truck never moved. "God dammit!" This was not how I wanted to spend the few hours I had before the clinic opened.

I kicked harder off the rocky slope, swinging closer but still not quite reaching the truck.

Mustering more strength than I thought my aching legs capable of, I pushed off the rocks one last time with all my might and managed to reach the door of the cab with the tips of my fingers. Clinging to the roof by my fingernails, I stared down through the branches to the wet ground so far below. My heart nearly stopped. *I hate heights.* I closed my eyes, calmed myself for a moment, and then forced myself to get back to work. Wrenching the door open, I could see a young woman slumped over the steering wheel, her long blond hair streaked with blood and hanging down toward the windshield.

I didn't have time to take a good look, but I could see the blood had seeped from a laceration on her forehead. Her skin was pale, and she didn't move when I opened the door. The accident must have knocked her unconscious, but there was no time to really assess her condition. I had more urgent matters to worry about.

The truck teetered as it swung on its splintering perch. Another branch cracked, and a limb popped free from the trunk. It fell to the ground, leaving the tons of twisted steel even less secure. For a moment, I held my breath, certain we were both about to plummet to our deaths. Miraculously, it seemed to be holding.

Sweating, I took the tail of the rope I had knotted around my waist and hurriedly wrapped it around hers, tying her close to me. I unbuckled her seatbelt, pulled her from the truck, and held her tight against my chest. In midair, we swung free in the silence, and I couldn't believe we were both still in one piece. Then the truck tipped, more limbs gave way in a deafening chorus of cracks and pops, and the whole truck crashed down through the branches. Tumbling in a crumpled heap down the cliff face, the violent mess crashed to the deep ravine far below.

Suspended at the end of my calf rope, we bumped into

the cold, jagged rock, safely above the wreckage. As I shook my head and thanked my lucky stars, I became aware of how limp she was. Her body was a dead weight. The only thing holding us up was the rope tied to the mangled rail above us.

I steeled myself and began the long climb, pulling us hand by hand up the rope. My feet steadied us on the rocks, and my shoulders screamed with the added weight of her. Finally, I got a hand on the rail and hauled myself up over it, pulling her up behind me. There, on the wet pavement, I sat gasping for breath with the broken woman in my arms.

Chapter Two

Paige

The light hit my eyes like bright shards of glass. That's the first and only thing I knew when I woke up.

Next came the agony. Brilliant pain shot through every part of me all at once. The bones in my hands, feet, legs, and arms felt broken clean, snapped in two. When I moved to see what strange shape I might be twisted into, a burning ache wrapped around my torso from the right side to the left.

"Mother of God!" I cried as I grabbed my ribs. *What the hell happened to me?*

Hidden behind an unbearable sterile light, a gentle voice spoke as though its owner had heard my thoughts. "You've been in an accident. You need to lie still."

I didn't recognize the warm, soothing voice, but its kind, authoritative richness had an instant calming effect on me. "God?" I whispered.

The voice laughed. "Not quite." I heard the faint sound of boots on tile approaching me, and then the voice was at my side. "My name is Josh Dalton. I'm a veterinarian."

"A veterinarian?" I tried to heave myself upright from whatever stiff surface I was laid out on, but I barely managed to push myself up an inch before my arms buckled and I collapsed with a thud to the back of my head. "Owww."

A firm hand settled on my shoulder, not to restrain me—clearly, I wasn't going anywhere—but in a misguided attempt to comfort me. "I'm what you get when you flip your truck off the road at four in the morning in the middle of nowhere."

"The middle of nowhere?" *Damn it!* I couldn't remember why I'd been on the road or where I was heading, but I knew I'd been trying to get somewhere. *Hadn't I?* I forced my eyes open, but in the white light, everything was a blur. "Where am I?"

"My clinic," the voice said.

I groaned as I tried to rub the ache from my head. "Where is that?"

"Whisper Cove."

I turned my head and looked up at the man by my side. In the light, I couldn't see the details of his face, but I could tell he was tall with thick arms and broad shoulders. *You might be able to outrun him,* I thought, *but you'd never be able to fight him. Not without a weapon.* Turning my head to scan my surroundings for anything I could stab or clobber him with, my blurry vision would only show me vague impressions and shapes.

My sense of smell, however, was working perfectly. The voice was surrounded by the scent of cashmere, vanilla, leather, wet dog, and a little bit of manure, altogether creating a repulsive and comforting bouquet.

"What is it?" His voice was so soft and easy it made me ashamed for even considering assaulting him.

"Where is Whisper Cove?" I asked.

"Where is it?" He shook his head, I assumed in disbelief. "It's about ten miles east of Route 1 and thirty miles south of the border."

"Mexico?" A smile spread across my face. I didn't know

why, exactly. I just knew Mexico was different from wherever I'd been, and that made it something to be happy about.

"The Canadian border," he said. "You really *are* lost, aren't you? You couldn't get farther from Mexico without leaving the country." He paused and his fuzzy head tilted. "Is that what you were trying to do? Leave the country?"

"No." I lied. Well, it wasn't *really* a lie. I had no idea what I'd been trying to do. "I don't know." My hand found my throbbing forehead and rubbed, but only for a second before my fingers touched a split in my skin that sent fiery pain through my brain and down my face. A whimper escaped me. "I can't remember."

"That's okay. That's normal. You took a hit to the head. It will come back to you."

"Will my vision come back?!" Tears leaked from the corners of my eyes, and I began to pant as panic hit me. "Everything's cloudy."

"Shhh..." His hand caressed my shoulder. "It will all come back. I gave you some fentanyl for the pain. You were moaning. I may have given you a little too much. I treat more horses than humans. Sorry."

His apology only made me sob harder. "What is this place?"

"You're in the back room of my clinic."

"You brought me back to your place? Why didn't you call an ambulance?! What?! Were you drunk when you hit me?!"

He pulled his hand from my shoulder and took a step back. "I didn't hit you." He didn't sound angry, but his voice was suddenly stern instead of kind. "I *found* you. Your truck was hanging in the trees on the wrong side of the guard rail off Shipwreck Road."

"Shipwreck…?" I shut my eyes tight and shook my head as I tried to make sense of it all. "Why didn't you call for help?!"

He took a deep, patient breath. "Because around here, I *am* the help. It's a long way to the nearest hospital."

"You should have taken me there anyway." I wiped the tears from my eyes. "Am I your prisoner?"

"No," he grumbled. "You're just the latest in a long line of dumb mistakes."

His boots squeaked as he turned his back and began to walk away.

"Wait!" I cried. Suddenly, the thought of being without him terrified me more than the thought of being held captive.

The tall man stopped, and I could see his head turn to the side like he was looking back over his shoulder at me. "What?"

"I—I'm..." *Sorry. Say you're sorry.* "I'm cold."

The figure turned and the sound of metal scraping metal filled the room as he opened the door of what I guessed was a cabinet. When he turned back to me, I could see the outline of a blanket in his hands, and above that, the shape of his face was growing clearer. His hair was light brown and the stubble on his jaw and cheeks matched it perfectly. Without another word, he spread the blanket over me. He was just close enough for me to see his light blue eyes.

"I'm scared," I whispered. "I don't know what happened."

He swallowed back his annoyance. "Don't be. I'm vet, but I'm still a doctor." When the blanket was tucked tight around me, he looked down into my eyes. "Let's try again. Hi, I'm Josh. What's your name?"

"Hi, Josh. I'm..." I stared back at him with an empty head and big, pleading eyes. "I'm..."

Josh

"I'm… I'm…" her wide green eyes stared up at me, unseeing. "I… I don't know… Who am I?"

I couldn't hide my smile, but I tried to hold back a chuckle. "I don't know. You're supposed to tell me. What do you remember?" I stepped away to wash my hands and dried them on a soft, well-worn clinic towel.

"The road… and then something… something big…. I tried to stop…. and… owww." She grabbed her head, but winced when she brushed against the neat stitches I had put in her scalp just minutes earlier.

"Hey, hey." I put a hand on her shoulder. "Just take it easy." She struggled to sit up, swinging her legs over the edge of the stainless steel exam table.

"I need to…" Her head rolled on her shoulders as a seasick expression overtook her. "I need to go."

"You're not going anywhere just yet." I caught her before she slid from the table. "Can I call someone for you? A husband? A boyfriend?" I let the question hang in the air, and she just shook her head, her eyes flicking back and forth between me and the door.

"Look, I need to open the clinic, and I need you out of my exam room. There's a cot in the back. I use it sometimes when I need to stay overnight and keep an eye on one of my patients. I can have the sheriff come over and talk to you."

"NO!" she scrambled back away from me on the table.

"Okay, okay." I backed away with my hands up. "No sheriff. But I really need to open the clinic. You can't stay here in this room, but you can come back to my office where it's a little more comfortable. There's a cot and a pillow and everything." I looked down at my watch. "You decide. I've got a Pomeranian and her owner coming in for a teeth cleaning in fifteen minutes, and neither one will be happy to wait."

She whimpered, craning her head to look around the exam room.

"Come on." I held out my hand. "Let me get you comfortable. You can take a shower and clean up."

Slowly, she gave me her trembling hand. Her fingers were so cold, I instinctively wrapped my big calloused hand around them to share some body heat. I helped her off the table, wrapped an arm around her waist, and she leaned into me, limping on weak and shaky legs all the way down the hall to the back room.

"Thank you." She looked up at me as we stopped in front of the bathroom.

"You want to get cleaned up?"

She nodded, wobbled on her feet, and grabbed the door frame. "Can you?"

"Yeah. Here you go." I guided her in, and she sat on the closed toilet lid. "You need any help?"

"No, no. I can do it." She took a deep breath in through her teeth as her chest expanded.

"All right. I'll be just outside if you need anything. I'm going to get ready to open." I didn't like leaving her, so I didn't go far. Stopping just out of her line of sight, I leaned against the wall. I heard her whimpering as she shuffled around and the sound her clothes falling to the floor. Then, like it or not, I had to go prepare for my first patient of the day.

Back in the exam room, I rummaged through the cabinets, setting out my supplies, and grumbled to myself as I tried to stay conscious. “Not a single minute of sleep.” Washing my hands, I splashed some cold water on my face to wake myself up.

"OH!"

Her cry echoed down the clinic hall, and I ran from the exam room to the bathroom in back, expecting to find her bleeding on the floor. When I got there, however, she was upright and okay… sort of.

I paused at the door, able to see her through the crack as she leaned against the porcelain sink in nothing but her white cotton panties. Her arms supported all her weight as she stared at herself in the mirror. Her green eyes were wide with shock.

Seeing she was fine, I turned away, but not before the vision of her imprinted itself on my brain. Turning my back, I couldn't shake away the sight of her lightly tanned skin or the smooth curve of her cheek that stretched down to her graceful neck. Her bare back tapered down to a narrow waist and flared back out to rounded hips. Her long legs went on for miles, taking up residence in the front of my consciousness. I hated myself for my visceral reaction to seeing her, but a long time had passed since I'd been with a woman. Most nights, I fell exhausted into a dreamless sleep.

That vision of her stuck with me. It made me want to help her even more, but not because of my attraction. In addition to her perfection, I saw the bruises, the vivid black stretching around her ribs, the marks from the seatbelt that had saved her life, and lacerations all over her lovely skin. If she wasn't willing to deal with the sheriff yet, I could at least care for her injuries while her head cleared up. I could tend her body that day while her mind rested for a few hours. I needed to know who she was, where she was from, and what had her running scared. *She* needed to know too.

"Hey, toss your clothes out," I called through the gap in the slightly open door. "I'll give you some clean scrubs until I get them washed." I heard the shower turn on, and then everything landed with a thump at my feet in the hall.

Quickly glancing at my watch, I was glad I didn't have time to stand around watching her through the crack in the door. I only had ten minutes before Mrs. Preston would be banging on the door with Muffy under her arm. I gathered her things from the floor and carried them to the wash on the other side of the clinic.

She'd been wearing a purple blouse and a pair of jeans. I stood at the washer, staring up at the soap and supplies my receptionist kept on a shelf over the laundry. It was a job I was entirely unprepared for. In addition to answering the phone, smiling at clients, and keeping the whole office organized, Chloe took care of all my dirty clothes. Once a week, I'd haul a couple laundry bags in, and she'd magically make them all fresh and clean again. Since she'd left, I'd been stuffing all my clothes in together and washing them on cold with a cup full of whatever bottle I happened to grab. Looking down at the silky blouse in my hands, I had a feeling it required a more delicate approach. Unfortunately, I didn't have one.

I tossed the blouse in and was stuffing her jeans in after it, when I heard something crinkle. I reached my hand in the pocket and pulled out a crumpled receipt. It was so faded I couldn't make anything out except part of the signature at the bottom. "Paige...," it read in neat, clean cursive letters before the handwriting faded toward the edge of the slip. *Is that who she is?*

Chapter Three

Paige

The reflection in the mirror stole my breath away. It was strange—not awful or frightening— but not pleasing, though I'm sure it could have been worse. It was entirely foreign to me. I recognized the features as familiar, like I'd seen them before, but I felt no ownership of them.

The long, blond hair framed a tanned face. Some of the features were delicate, like the slender nose and high cheekbones. Others, the bright green eyes and full lips, were bold and striking. Maybe I should have been alarmed by the dried blood splattered all over that face, but I felt nothing. I couldn't see the woman in the mirror as me. She was a stranger staring back at me from a looking glass. Her wounds and bruises made me sad for her, but they weren't mine.

"Hey, toss your clothes out," the man said. "I'll give you some clean scrubs until I get them washed."

My vision had clear, and this time when I looked, I could see him. He was standing sideways at the door, his head turned away to keep from seeing my nakedness. My eyes fell upon my own body, and a gasp escaped my lips. A dark bruise crossed from the right side of my waist, up between my breasts, and ended at my left shoulder, bearing a striking resemblance to a seatbelt. My arms were covered in tiny lacerations and spots of purple bruises. I couldn't see beneath my underwear, but I could feel the dull ache of more bruises.

Tearing my eyes away from the ruins of my own body, I turned the shower on, took off my underwear, and threw all my clothes toward the stranger in the door. When they landed at his feet, he calmly bent over and picked them up. Then he shut the door, and I could hear his boots moving away.

The closed door frightened me. I was standing naked in a strange room with no clothes, no escape route, and no idea who I was. I didn't even know if the big man with the warm voice was my savior or captor. Maybe it was a good thing the pain meds he'd given me prevented my fear from growing into full-blown panic. Otherwise, the persistent urge to run would have driven me naked out into the streets… if there were streets. I didn't know that either.

I held my hand under the spray to test the water temperature and then stepped into the narrow shower closing the curtain behind me. There was a bottle of men's shampoo-slash-body wash in the shower caddy. When I popped the top open and sniffed, it smelled just like the gentle voice with the fuzzy head— cashmere, vanilla, and leather. All that was missing was the hint of wet dog and cow stool.

Given my state, I had to assume I was safe—at least from him. Soaking my hair under the hot spray, I poured the soap into my hand and rubbed it gently over my torso, carefully washing away the dirt and dried blood while avoiding direct contact with my wounds. The fresh stitches on my forehead stung where the water hit them, and I didn't dare wash my face for fear I'd bring back the awful pain I'd felt in the other room. Although, I wasn't really in any pain anymore. Whatever he'd given me, it left me feeling warm and numb, and I found myself swaying blissfully under the falling water until the shower finally ran cold.

I hadn't heard Josh come in, but when I turned the water off and stepped out of the shower, I found a fresh towel and clean blue scrubs waiting for me. There were no underpants, so I dried as well as I could and slipped into the clean clothes without them. They were ridiculously large on me, clearly sized for him, but they were well broken-in and soft, and they made me feel safe… and sleepy.

I remembered he'd told me there was a cot waiting for me back in his office. Staggering, I opened the bathroom door and poked my head out. There was a long hallway that extended right and left from where I stood. To my left, the sound of people talking and animals whimpering echoed through what must have been his lobby or an exam room. To my right, the hall stretched down to quiet, empty doorways.

I turned right, and with my hand on the wall to steady myself, wandered dreamily toward the back of the clinic. The very last door was open, and inside, a neatly made cot with fresh sheets, a blanket, and a pillow sat opposite a big wood desk and matching file cabinets. It was all I could manage to cross the room and collapse onto the small bed before my eyes closed and I was fast asleep.

I don't know how long I was out—an hour, maybe more. When I finally opened my eyes, the room was quiet. The man, Josh, must have shut the door sometime after I'd fallen asleep.

The effect of whatever drugs he'd given me was still strong enough to keep the pain at bay, but it had tapered off enough for the reality of my situation to come crashing down on me. Whatever had chased me to the middle of nowhere—Whisper Cove, Josh had said—well, I had no reason to believe it had stopped chasing me, which meant I should still be running.

I sat up in bed and looked around the floor for my shoes, but realized I wouldn't recognize them if I saw them. At the same time, I tried to make sense of my location. Josh had said

I was thirty miles south of the US-Canadian border and just a few miles east of Route 1. Route 1 ran up and down the east coast from the tip of Florida to Maine, so I had to be on the coast of northern Maine, right? But was I running to Canada, or from it? I didn't know.

It seemed like any move I made was as likely to be the wrong one as the right one. If I ran, I could just as easily be running toward danger as away from it. The only thing I knew for sure was that, wherever I'd come from, it wasn't Whisper Cove. That meant I was already in the only place I knew in the whole world to be safe.

But I couldn't stay there forever. I needed to keep moving. I just had to figure out which way to go.

Pushing myself up off the cot, my slightly numb feet landed on the cold tile floor. My balance was steadier than before, and I didn't need to brace myself against the walls or furniture, as long as I took it slowly. At a snail's pace, I made my way to the closed door and pulled it open. The smells and sounds of a whole different world flooded in around me.

The canine scent was back and joined by another equally animal but unknown odor. I could hear a cat howling and a dog yipping as voices tried to calm them.

"You hush, Buddy," someone said.

"Minnie, you be nice!" said another.

In my bare feet, I advanced down the hall to the source of the sounds and odors. The way dead-ended at an unattended reception desk and a half-full lobby. To avoid the people and animals, I stayed out of sight, just peeking in and watching the chaos.

A chubby woman holding a cat carrier leaned toward an older man gripping a golden retriever's leash. "Mack, that Daisy of yours is going to pop any day now."

"Already did," the man said with a smile. "Poor old Doc spent the night in my barn to make sure we didn't lose one."

"Congratulations, Buddy!" The woman reached over and

pet the golden's head. "He's the proud father of how many this time?"

"Seven, but it would have been six if Doc hadn't been there."

~

~

Josh

I shut and locked the front door after the last patient of the day, Jo-Jo, a 6 month old German shepherd with a taste for tube socks, left wagging her tail goodbye. It took more time to console her owners than it did to give her a laxative and wait for the offending footwear to move through her system. In such a small town, emergencies were my bread and butter, but they never came at convenient times. Before the German shepherd, it was a year-old kitten in for a checkup after her spaying. Before the kitten, a hedgehog that didn't want to eat.

I'd even had a human patient that day. Avery Gray had burned herself during a minor kitchen fire at her bar just down the street. It was the latest in a long line of mishaps that kept her and her bar in constant need of repair. I'd cleaned her up, applied some burn cream, wrapped her arm, and sent her back to work. I wasn't licensed to treat humans, but her injuries were a matter of simple first aid. With Paige, on the other hand, I knew I'd crossed a line.

I should have called for an ambulance there at the scene. I should never have brought her back to the clinic. I shouldn't have stitched her up, and I sure as hell shouldn't have given her pain medication. *What the hell were you thinking?* I guess I wasn't thinking at all.

You need to go check on Paige. I thought of her as 'Paige' now. It had been hours since I'd last looked in on her, and she'd been sound asleep, curled up on the cot and buried under the old horse blanket I used when I stayed over. She'd been resting, but with the little gasps and whimpers, I wouldn't call it restful.

"It's Josh," I called, straightening myself up as I moved down the hall toward the back room. "You doing okay?" I stopped by the laundry to drop a load of dirty towels in the washer, dumped a cup of whatever in, and started the machine. Grabbing her clothes from the dryer, I thought about folding them for her, but that was also above my domestic skill level.

With her clothes bunched up in one arm, I stood outside the closed door to my office, listening for movement, but all was still. I knocked on the door and waited for her to answer. "Hey, it's Josh." I cleared my throat. "I'm the guy who—"

"I know who you are," I heard softly through the door. "Come in."

I opened it to find her standing by the window, gazing out at the kennel run behind the clinic. Late afternoon sunlight shone through the light bloodless waves of her blond locks. And though she looked ridiculous with my enormous scrubs hanging off her, it was an adorable ridiculous. I wanted her to turn and look at me so I could see her face, but she didn't. She just stared out in silence.

"No guests at the inn," I said, chuckling nervously.

Finally, she turned and squinted at me. "What?"

I took a few steps toward her, gesturing out the window. "No dogs in the kennel." Without a word, she turned back toward the window. "Thank God." I said, "The last thing I need tonight is a bunch of animals requiring 24-hour observation."

She nodded.

"You ready to go talk to the sheriff?" I asked, handing her the clean clothes.

"What? No!" She clutched them close, knuckles white. "No sheriff! No police!"

"Come on, Paige—"

"Paige? Who's Paige?" She looked up at me, her green eyes big and wide, swimming with tears. My heart sank at the sight of them.

"You are... I think." I dug into my pocket and pulled out the receipt from her jeans. "I found this in your things when I washed them."

She reached eagerly for the scrap of paper and devoured it with her eyes, turning it over and over. "But, that's all it says?"

"Yeah. I'm sorry." I sat gingerly on the cot. "That's all I found. Well, and fifteen cents." I cocked an eyebrow. "Does that sound like you? Are you Paige?"

She let the crumpled paper fall like a broken feather to the floor and turned her sad eyes back out the window. "I don't know. I don't know who I am."

"Well, is it okay to call you Paige for now? You need a name, and it's a good one."

She shrugged. "As good as any other, I guess."

"You don't remember anyone at all, Paige? No friends or family you should call?"

Her lip trembled, and her voice was barely more than a breath. "No."

I sat still and watched her for a moment. It was hard to imagine what she was going through. I felt panic when I even lost my keys, but she'd lost everything… even herself. She had no one to reach out to, but I knew someone, somewhere was looking for her. Tall, curvy, and stunning even covered with cuts and bruises—someone was missing her. An evil little part of me was glad she didn't want to be found.

"Come on." I came to my feet. "If you won't let me take you to Sheriff Fox, I guess you're coming home with me."

She looked up at me with a strange mix of worry and relief. "But…"

"Paige, I'm dead on my feet. I haven't seen my bed since five a.m. yesterday. I'm too old to pull two all-nighters in a row. I've got a spare bedroom and an extra frozen dinner in the fridge." Sticking my hands in my pocket to resist the urge to touch her, I nodded at the door. "Come on. My truck's out back."

Josh, what the hell are you doing? This is stupid. She needs real help. You're gonna lose your license.

Ignoring my inner voice of reason, I walked out to the hall. "Go ahead and change. I'll wait out front."

I sat in the lobby, twirling my keys around my finger until the door opened and she made her way out front. I had to suck in a breath at the sight of her. The figure that had been hidden under baggy scrubs was on full display in snug jeans that cupped her ass and the purple blouse that hung over her breasts. My body reacted again to the sight of her, reminding me of the glimpse I'd caught in the bathroom. It was a crying shame when she pulled her form jacket over everything.

Stop it. I worked too long and too hard. I had no time for women. *Especially needy women with problems.* I had my own needs and problems. I needed to find someone to run the front desk until Chloe came back from maternity leave. I needed a big animal vet at least part-time. The pets of Whisper Cove dominated my attention, leaving me little to devote to all the livestock in need of care. Besides, I was getting a little old for pulling calves in the middle of the night.

I respectfully turned my gaze away, but I could feel her eyes on me, and I wondered if she liked what she saw. *What does a woman with no memory think of a man who smells like dog and drives a ten-year-old pickup that hasn't been cleaned in nine and a half years?* I'm sure I looked like hell after being up 36 hours straight and climbing halfway down a mountain to rescue her from what would have been certain death. *She's probably not thinking of you at all.*

I sighed and locked the clinic door behind us before leading her to the truck and helping her into the passenger seat. I drove in silence the half-hour home, watching her profile from the corner of my eye. I could tell this woman was going to turn my life upside down.

Chapter Four

Paige

The rusty old truck rattled as Josh drove the crumbling back roads to his place. Neither one of us said much. He could barely keep his eyes open and his head up, and I was too busy imagining all the horrible things strangers do to young women who are foolish enough to take rides from them. This was more than just a ride, but what choice did I have? Given that he was literally the only person I knew in the whole world, the fact that I'd known him less than 24 hours, most of which I'd slept through, seemed insignificant.

He turned left, and the pot-holed pavement gave way to dirt and gravel. I made sure to keep track of all the rights, lefts, and landmarks we passed along the way. If he turned into a monster in the privacy of his own home, running would be my best chance at survival. He was at least a half a foot taller and 75 pounds of muscle bigger than me. He could have snapped me like a twig, but he'd have to catch me first.

As we rode along for what seemed like forever, my fear gave way to admiration of our surroundings. There were so many plants and trees, and all of it seemed so new and exotic. Rolling hills lifted us higher and higher until it seemed we were driving atop mountains. To my left and right, vast fields were draped in red and magenta shrubs surrounded by towering pines of darkest green. Trees—more than I'd ever imagined existed—seemed painted in crimson, orange, and gold. Massive boulders sat wherever nature had left them. And above it all, a brilliant pink and lavender sky grew brighter and brighter as it fought back dusk. It was breathtaking… and utterly foreign to me.

We reached a long stretch of flat land where there was nothing but nature and a big white farmhouse in the distance. Josh's eyes locked on the far-off dwelling, and I could tell it was his. Beneath my horror at the isolation and impossibly long trek between me and the safety of civilization, I almost wished it was mine too.

As we rode up the long dirt driveway, I half expected a handful of big, yellow dogs to come running to greet their master, but they didn't. The land was beautiful, and the house was straight out of a New England fantasy, but it was a lonely and deserted fantasy.

"Let me get that door for you," he said as the truck rolled to a stop in front of the house. "It sticks, and your arm needs to heal." He climbed out from behind the wheel, came around the front, and opened my door. Then he stood there, his hand held out. "It's a big step down." There was no sparkle of flirtation in his eyes, just exhausted concern.

I took his big hand and leaned against him as I slid to the ground. When I was safely on my feet, he shut the door, turned, and walked toward the house. I followed, looking around at all the empty spaces where flowers should have grown, chairs should have rocked, and tire swings should have hung from a massive tree. A shiny red Mustang, an old one, sat off to one side of the driveway. Tall grass and weeds grew up around the wheels that clearly hadn't move in a while.

Josh's world, with its wrap-around porch and gorgeous view, was like a model home—

—a testament to unmet potential.

The front steps creaked as we made our way up. Josh opened the door and stood aside to let me in. I looked at him, unable to stifle a laugh. "You don't lock it?"

He wrinkled his brow like I'd said something ridiculous. "You're letting the heat out." Taking my cue, I stepped past him through the door.

The front room was so shadowy I smelled the house before I saw it. The fragrance of cedar, old books, and firewood filled my senses. I drew a deep breath and enjoyed the strange sensation of *home* that followed. I was sure, whatever my home actually was, it didn't smell like that. No, this was like coming home to the place you should have always been but never were. The only thing missing was the scent of fresh-baked pie and pot roast.

Josh flipped a switch, and antique wall sconces filled the room with a yellow glow, revealing a worn couch and chairs, family portraits on dark green walls, and a braided wool rug over an aged hardwood floor. There were chests and lamps, handmade furniture, and books—more books than I could have accumulated in a lifetime.

"You like to read?" I grinned and teased.

Josh shut the door behind him and set his leather bag down on the floor beside it. "Yup. Just like my parents and my grandparents…" he sighed, "...and my great grandparents." He pointed to the overflowing shelves. "This is a four-generation collection. There are shelves all through the house. I come from a long line of nerds."

"I guess you do." I walked over to the shelves and ran my fingers gently along the dusty spines. "May I touch them?"

He nodded as he passed me and disappeared into another room. "That's what they're there for. Read up!"

As he opened cupboard doors and moved plates around in

what must have been the kitchen, my eyes landed on a particularly beautiful volume. The blue leather spine was intricately decorated with gold scrolling that still shined in the light despite its age. I pulled it down from the shelf and studied the cover. Running my fingers over the lovely gold inlay, I whispered, "A Midsummer Night's Dream."

The binding crackled as I gently turned the cover open. Inside, a dried and faded red rose lay pressed between a layer of tissue and a blank page, upon which a note had been inscribed. "Darling Mary," it read, "I hope this tale brings you as much magic as you've brought me. Yours eternally —Joshua."

The inscription alone made my heart flutter. It couldn't have been written by the Josh who had rescued me; the ink was old and the letters were perfectly slanted, curled, and uniform like calligraphy. I imagine Joshua may have been his father or his grandfather, maybe his great grandfather. And Mary—well, I envied her.

"Salisbury steak or lasagna?" I looked up from the book to see Josh standing in the doorway, a frozen boxed dinner in each hand. "Sorry, but I don't get a lot of time to cook." He shrugged. "Or shop."

"Lasagna. Thank you." As he turned back to the kitchen, I closed the book, careful not to crush the fragile rose. I slipped it back in its place on the shelf and followed after him.

That's not real, a voice inside me warned. I squeezed my fist, forcing my fingernails sharply into the tender palms of my hands and focused on the pain. *People don't love like that anymore. That was written a hundred years ago by a dead man to a dead woman. You'll be dead too if you don't keep running.*

Josh

"Mmmmh…" I groaned as I pulled a pillow over my head to drown out the racket. My foggy brain couldn't make sense of it. It felt like I'd barely fallen asleep before it started. My eyelids fluttered, and I rolled over to see the big red numbers on the clock. 3:07 am. "Nooooooo…"

After my culinary feast of microwaved Salisbury steak washed down with an icy cold Miller Lite, I'd taken a quick shower and fallen face first into bed, wrapping myself in the crazy old patchwork quilt I hadn't taken time to straighten the last time I'd left it.

The sun hadn't even set yet, but I'd fallen fast asleep. I didn't give much thought to my guest either. I'd just pointed her in the direction of the guest room, given her instructions on how to coax hot water out of the finicky pipes, and left her to her own devices.

I hope the phone didn't wake her.

"The phone!" *That's* what the godawful racket had been. My cell phone rang merrily on the nightstand next to me. I grabbed it and tried to yawn my way to consciousness. "Hullo?"

"Doc!" A frantic voice came over the line. "Doc, you gotta get back out here."

"Mack? Is that you? What's going on?"

"It's the runt. It's breathing, but it's not moving. Ma's all upset. Daisy keeps crying and licking it. Stopped nursing this afternoon. I tried to do that thing you showed me, with the rag and milk, but it didn't work. You gotta do something."

"Mack, calm down." I had already swung my legs over the side of the bed, my feet automatically seeking my fuzzy slippers as they met the cold floor. "I'll be there soon. Keep it warm and keep drizzling the milk as best you can." I didn't hold out much hope, but I couldn't tell him that. Mack had a soft heart, and I loved him for it. Animals were my life, and the people I liked best were the ones that loved their animals too. And who knew—maybe the runt would surprise me.

I picked up my dirty jeans from the day before, not even bothering to search for clean ones, and pulled a long sleeved shirt and a pair of boxer briefs from the basket of clean clothes next to the dresser. My jeans, well broken in, slid up over my thighs like they were made for me. I pulled the shirt over my head as I tiptoed down the steps trying not to wake Paige.

Scribbling a hasty note, I explained I was heading out on a call, folded it, and anchored it with the empty fruit bowl sitting forgotten in the center of the kitchen table. My boots stood ready by the door, and I was dressed and on my way in under five minutes, my routine perfected after hundreds of midnight calls. Grabbing the keys from the hook by the door, I set off.

Chapter Five

Paige

Moonlight spilled in through the wavy window panes and sheer curtains, casting soft blue over the bedroom. Sleepless, I studied my surroundings—the aged family photos, the antique dresser, the stenciled ladder-back rocking chair—and found the sense of permanence they offered somewhat comforting. Knowing one of the matriarch's of his family had sewn each green and blue patch by hand made the quilt feel like an embrace, and I held it tight like a security blanket.

I didn't know Josh. We'd barely spoken since I'd opened my eyes. He didn't know me either. *I* didn't even know me. Still, the faint sound of his breathing in the next room reminded me I wasn't alone, that my protector was nearby. I guess when you desperately need a hero, you'll attach that title to anyone who'll wear it. He hadn't turned me away or betrayed me when I begged him not to call the sheriff even though I couldn't give him a reason why. In my desperate state, that made him my champion. Even so, I was panicked and fighting to remain still while every part of me wanted to run.

It's okay. You're okay. He's right in the next room. He'll hear you if you scream. He won't let anyone hurt you.

I repeated those words in my head over and over, but while they kept me from bolting out the door, they did nothing to bring me peace. The night seemed endless. If not for the sound of his breathing and the *tick-tick-tick* of the clock, I would have thought time itself stood still.

The house and the land around it was so quiet when I heard the buzzing of his phone, I nearly jumped out of my skin. My heart pounded in my chest as I listened to the squeaking of his bed springs and his voice as he answered.

"Hullo?" he said dreamily. "Mack? Is that you? What's going on?" He paused, and in the resulting quiet, my stomach turned as I imagined I was the subject of their conversation. "Mack, calm down. I'll be there as soon as I can. Keep it warm and keep drizzling the milk as best you can." By the time he hung up, I was too confused to make sense of it.

A moment later, I heard Josh's bare feet plodding softly down the hall and then down the staircase. I sat up in bed, listened for a moment, and climbed out from under the quilt to chase after him. In my underwear and a borrowed t-shirt, I raced down the hall toward the stairs, but it was too late. I hadn't even reached the top step when I heard the front door open and shut. By the time I reached the bottom, his headlights shined yellow in through the front windows and grew dimmer and dimmer as he backed down the long dirt driveway.

Alone in the dark, I held tight to the bannister as my legs trembled beneath me. I panted, and my lower lip began to quiver. Unable to stop them, tiny terrified whimpers escaped me like those of a frightened child. I collapsed back on the steps, covered my face with my hands, and sobbed.

I couldn't remember ever being alone like that before. The

house was empty. The yard around it was empty. The forest beyond, well, I *hoped* it was empty. I hadn't seen a phone or a TV when we came in, and I assumed Josh had taken his cell phone with him. Whatever was hunting me, if it found me, would have all the time and space in the world to do whatever it wanted to me. No one would hear me cry for help. I was a sitting duck in that old farmhouse, and it was only a matter of time before whoever was chasing me found me.

Like a hand to my back, fear brought me to my feet and sent me running to the kitchen. I opened and slammed shut all the drawers, but found only a hundred years of accumulated junk and a mismatched collection of harmless flatware. Josh may never have cooked, but there were three generations of women before him, and I knew at least one of them must have carved a turkey in her life. I spun in place in the center of the hardwood floor, eying every corner of my surroundings.

Finally, I caught sight of it sitting quietly against the wall by the sugar, flour, and canisters. The knife block was faded with age, its time-bleached wood blended seamlessly with the counter and cupboards. I grabbed the largest handle in the block and watched the moonlight shine off the long, wide blade as I pulled it from its slot. Holding it up for inspection, I reasoned that, though it wouldn't be as effective as a gun, it would stop any man dumb enough to come near me.

Is it a man I'm running from?

Knife in hand, I rushed back to the stairs and up the steps to the guest room. I climbed onto the bed and pulled the quilt up around me for protection. With my head resting on my knees and the knife securely in my grip, I stared out the wavy glass at the empty field, the dark pines, and the black ocean far beyond. "Not here," I whispered.

Hopping out of bed, I paused for just a moment to grab my folded jeans from the rocking chair and then dashed for Josh's bedroom. It was on the other side of the hallway and offered a view of the road and driveway that I needed if I was going to see my enemy approaching. There was less light on that side of the house, but that only made it easier to see the world outside. I set the knife down just long enough to slip my jeans on and then crawled up on his bed.

I may have hoped we were in the middle of nowhere, far enough from civilization to prevent anyone from tracking us down, but I soon discovered the Daltons weren't the only ones crazy enough to plant themselves on a remote mountain. Surrounded by Josh's personal possessions, I was almost comforted enough to set the knife down and curl up in his blankets, but it's always when you let your guard down that danger presents itself. As I turned to place my weapon on the bedside table, a set of white headlights appeared on the distant road.

My pulse quickened, and my heart beat so hard I could hear its echo in the blood coursing through my ears. The driver must have had his high beams on because the light it cast spread far ahead of him and wide in all directions. At a curve in the road, the headlights shined on the house, through the old windows of Josh's bedroom, and set the lawn aglow. That glow only last a few seconds, but it was long enough for me to see my miracle, one I'd neglected to appreciate when we'd first arrived, sitting out on the edge of the lawn.

The headlights landed on the polished metal, making the surface shine in the darkness. It happened fast, but I saw chrome gleaming and the familiar curve of a windshield. *The car!* I had forgotten all about the cherry red Mustang in the yard.

Hope replaced fear in my heart, and I leapt off the bed and raced to the stairs with the knife tight in my hold, flying down the steps two at a time. Throwing the front door open, I stepped out onto the porch and stared at the outline of the dark shape.

Keys! Get the keys, Paige!

People hung their keys on hooks in their kitchens, didn't they? Visions of a hundred decorative key holders mounted by a hundred doors danced through my head. I ran to the kitchen and looked on every wall, but there was nothing—no keys and no phone.

I opened and shut the drawers again, this time looking for an old ring of keys he might have thoughtlessly dumped in with the restaurant menus and sewing kit but found nothing. I opened all the cupboards, hoping I'd find them dangling from a hook mounted on the inside of their doors, but I found only plates, bowls, and coffee cups. Frustrated, I leaned back against the counter and stared at the mess I'd made rummaging around. That's when I remembered.

If Josh didn't worry enough to lock his front door, he probably didn't worry enough to lock the car either. I picked up the knife and sprinted to the living room. Throwing the door open again, I held the knife flat against my chest and cautiously stepped out onto the porch. This time, I looked all around the yard and the shadows of the trees for anything that might be lying in wait to launch an attack. When I was certain I was alone, I raced down the steps and across the driveway.

I didn't stop to examine the vehicle—there was no time. I said a quick prayer and pulled on the door handle, and sure enough, the door popped open. Sliding in behind the wheel, I wondered if I knew how to hotwire a car and if it would be something I'd remember now. Fortunately, it didn't come to that.

Feeling around the steering column, my fingers touched something cold and hard dangling loose. The resulting jingle was unmistakable. I shook my head. Josh was so trusting he didn't even bother to take his keys from the ignition. I hated myself for being the one to teach him a lesson about protecting what he loved, but that car was my ticket to safety.

I turned the key, and a demented laugh escaped me when

the engine roared to life. It took a few moments of blindly patting at the dash, but my fingers eventually found the switch, and the headlights beamed in front of me, illuminating the entire farmhouse. Seeing it from the outside, my heart ached to leave it behind… but it only ached for a moment.

There were three pedals on the floor and a stick shift between the bucket seats, and the way my left foot found the clutch and my right hand found reverse, it was obvious I knew how to drive a stick shift. I hung my arm over the back of the passenger's seat and looked over my shoulder as I set the car moving backward toward the road. I turned onto the gravel, shifted into first gear, and with one last look at Josh's beautiful home, I sped off down the dirt road.

I didn't know where I was going, but I remembered Josh had taken a right, a left, two rights, and three lefts to get home that evening. It stood to reason three rights, two lefts, a right, and a left would get me back to the paved road. From there, I could go either way and end up either in Canada or on my way down south. I took the first right a couple miles down the road, then another and another.

Recognizing some familiar landmarks, a sign for McCormick's Blueberry Farm and the crooked steeple of a decaying church, I knew I was on the right path. Still, I felt that hand in my back, pressing me to go farther faster. That hand pushed harder when a set of headlights appeared in the rearview mirror.

"Fuck," I whispered. My eyes shifted nervously from the road to the mirror and back again, over and over. "Fuck, fuck, fuck." The lights were far apart, and I assumed it was a truck.

Is that Josh?

Uncertain who was behind me, whether they were coincidentally driving the same remote stretch of dirt as I was in the wee hours of the morning, or if they were pursuing me, I pressed my foot down on the gas. The engine roared and propelled me farther ahead. As I watched the lights in the rearview, I couldn't tell if they were falling behind or speeding up to catch me.

Miles passed beneath my wheels before it occurred to me that the best way to know if I was being followed was to turn off onto a side road and see if the lights behind me turned too. The first turn to present itself was a sharp left, and I took it at full speed, sending the rear end of the Mustang drifting around the front. Maintaining speed, I kept an eye on the mirror to see if the vehicle behind me did the same. Maybe they knew I had no chance of escaping because when they did finally turn the corner and appeared in the rearview again, it was at a slow, easy pace.

Damnit!

Tears welled up in my eyes and slid down my cheeks as panic gripped me once more. *They're coming for you,* I thought. A moment later, *Don't be crazy. It's a public road.* The only way to find out was to take another random turn, this time onto a smaller, less traveled road.

I drove a few miles with the headlights shining behind me before I spotted a narrow opening in the trees. Without slowing down, I turned right and the back spun around again. I could hear gravel kicking up, hitting the fenders as I pushed the car harder down the remote drive.

Holding my breath, I waited for the lights to appear behind me again, and they did, but only for a moment. The trailing vehicle passed by the turn I'd taken and kept moving down the road, away from me. When they were gone and only blackness remained, I slowed the car to a stop and caught my breath.

Oh, God.

I turned my head left and right, watching the tree limbs sway and the leaves quiver in the moonlight. Ahead, there was only darkness, and behind was the same. There were no houses or street lights, nothing to show me the way.

You took a left and a right to get here, so you need to take a right and a left to get back. Right? No. A left and a right to get back. Yes. No. But which left and which right?

I was lost and all turned around, but I didn't have time to be. Shifting into reverse, I turned in my seat and slowly backed down the way I'd come, guided only by the car's anemic back-up lights. It was slow work, and with every second that passed, my anxiety escalated. By the time I finally made it back to main road—well, the road I'd come from, anyhow—a soft cry marked my every breath.

I turned backwards, guessing which way I'd come, and slipped into first before my wheels even came to a stop. The car lurched, and I traveled deeper into the choking darkness. When I came to a spot that looked familiar, I turned left, wondering all the time if I should have turned right.

Hours seemed to pass that way, but I had no means of knowing how long I'd actually been driving or how far. Turn after turn, left and right and left, I had no idea where I was going. All the trees and fields looked the same in the moonlight. All the shadows seemed to lay in wait. Finally, a yellow light flashed to life on the fuel gage to the left of the speedometer, and I knew my race was over.

Before I could end up stranded on the side of a well-traveled road, where any predator could have found me, I turned onto a narrow path that was little more than tire tracks worn into grass. I drove that way until the path dead-ended at the edge of a stream. Under a starry sky, I shifted gears back to first, turn the key in the ignition, and the engine died with rumble.

Josh

I hit the brakes, and the car rolled to a stop just as the first rays of light streaked across the morning sky. Stretching, I tucked my passenger back in to my shirt and then climbed out of the truck gingerly, shutting the door behind me with a *click.*

With my hand still leaning against the closed door, my eyes peered across the top of the truck and came to rest on the empty spot in the yard. A perfect rectangle of dry yellow grass stood where my father's 1969 Ford Mustang Boss usually sat.

"Oh, Shit..." The first thought that crossed my mind was that it had been stolen. Sleepy little Whisper Cove had finally been discovered by the criminal element. Then I realized the more likely answer—the one who should have been asleep in the guest room where I'd left her. "What did you do, Paige?"

I groaned, opened the door, and climbed back into my truck. Still warm, the engine didn't hesitate before it revved back to life. Making a u-turn in the driveway, the sun popped up above the tree line in my rear view mirror as I pulled toward the road.

I dreaded to think what would happen to Paige on these back roads in the old Mustang. I'd barely gotten it running last summer, the powerful V8 engine was still finicky, and provided way too much power for someone unfamiliar with steep mountain roads. And, "Oh!" I leaned my head against the steering wheel for a moment before turning left out of the driveway, remembering I had drained most of the fuel in preparation for cleaning the tank. She couldn't have gotten far, but that also meant she could be stranded somewhere, anywhere within a twenty mile radius. That was a lot of mountain to cover.

I glanced down at the center console, snagged my cell phone resting in the cup holder, and hit the third number in my favorites.

It took her a few rings to answer before she grumbled, "Josh?"

"Hey, Avery, how is that hand doing?"

"It's healing up. What's going on?"

"Uh... nothing. I was just wondering if you had seen any

strangers wandering through town today?" If anyone had the latest info on newcomers, it would be Avery, town bartender, willing shoulder to cry on, and local information center.

"Today?" she grumbled.

"Right."

"*Today* today? Like the one where it's only five-thirty in the morning and my alarm doesn't go off for another two hours?"

Feeling like a giant ass, I shook my head. "Yeah, that's the one."

"Nope. Can't say I've seen anyone new today." On the other end of the line, something seemed to snap, and Avery woke right up. "Why? Have you been seeing strangers around?"

"No, Avery."

"You have something you should tell me, Josh?"

"No—"

"My kegs didn't just lose pressure on their own, you know."

"Avery, calm down—"

"Don't tell me to calm down, Josh! That's money I don't have to waste! Now if there's someone suspicious—"

"Avery! Calm down! It's nothing like that. Go back to sleep."

"You wouldn't lie to me, Josh…"

I focused my bleary eyes on the road ahead. "I never have."

"You wouldn't start…"

I shook my head. "Sorry to wake you up, Avery. Sweet dreams." I ended the call before she could ask me anymore questions. She was a good friend, but times like that, I was glad she was only a friend. Sure, she was a tall, sexy Amazon with long dark hair and a naughty smile, but she was also way more than I could handle. "Say hi to Caleb for me," I mumbled in the silence of the truck.

Patting the package tucked in my shirt, I kept my eyes

peeled for the cherry red paint of my Mustang. I drove for over an hour, up and down one back road after another, watching at every turn for skid marks, crushed grass, a break in the trees, anything that might indicate Paige had gone off the road.

Left, right, up, and down as the sun rose higher and higher and the day grew warmer. I pulled off to the side of the road after two hours to take the squirming bundle from my shirt. Mewling blindly, the tiny puppy opened its mouth, yawned with its little tongue extending and curling, and then closed its mouth and let out a squeak.

I rummaged through my bag on the seat next to me, finally finding a baby bottle and a can of puppy formula. The pup nursed with his paws kneading my thumb, and then we continued on.

The phone rang on the seat next to me, and I answered, expecting Avery. "You think of something?"

"Josh?" Instead of Avery's dulcet tones, a gruff male voice met my ears.

"Oh, sorry, Mack. What's up?"

"I'm just calling to check on the pup. Did he make it through the night?"

"He's still hanging in there." I reached in my shirt again, rubbing the rounded fuzzy belly of the sleeping puppy. Just over a day old, he was still no bigger than my hand.

"Okay, Doc," Mack said. "Just… just let me know if anything changes, okay?"

"I promise," I told him. Then I ended the call and continued searching for my missing beauty.

I came upon the turn off to one of my favorite fishing holes, a narrow path that was little more than tire tracks worn into grass. About a quarter mile in, the road stopped at edge of a swift flowing stream. There, the roots of a large white birch formed a hollow, and the deeper water beneath it sheltered trout and the occasional bass. On the rare occasion I had an afternoon off, I would sometimes bring a lawn chair and my fishing pole and drop a line, hoping to catch dinner. Most times, I came home empty handed, but the afternoon passed peacefully.

This time, instead of trout, I found Dad's Mustang with the door standing wide open.

My heart raced as I stepped out of the truck, looking around for any sign of Paige. When I got to the car, the keys still dangled from the ignition. The car looked fine, but she was nowhere to be found. I stood on the tips of my toes, looking around at the endlessly moving trees, water, and shadows, but I still couldn't see her anywhere.

The pup slept sweetly tucked inside my warm shirt. I could feel his heart fluttering, and he occasionally sneezed, his whiskers tickling my chest. I cast my gaze about, finally spotting a footprint following the water's edge.

“Paige!" I called, my boots squishing in the mud. "Paige, where are you?"

In the high fifties, I would have enjoyed the morning more had I not been so worried about her wandering around injured with total amnesia. Who knew what would happen to her out in the woods alone. Moose, bears, the occasional wolf or coyote—the Maine woods were no place for the unprepared. Also, having a clinic to run made the whole game of hide and seek that much more stressful.

"Paige?"

A low whimpering led me to a stand of turning maples. In the center, leaning against a slab of granite, Paige sat barefoot with tears streaming from her eyes, her face pale, scared. A warrior, beautiful in her pain, she crouched with one of my large kitchen knives clutched to her chest, determined to defend herself.

Chapter Six

Paige

He found me.

At first, he was just a pair of lips—thin, chapped, and twisted in an expression of such rage it chilled me to the bone. He was saying something, but I couldn't hear the words. Anyway, I didn't need sound to know they were full of maniacal hate and determination, both terrifying and directed straight at me.

There was no hit to the head or familiar object that magically jogged my memory. His face appeared in my mind of its own accord. It was as though his pursuit extended beyond wheels and roads, beyond the physical world, and into my mind. And he caught me.

I was so frightened by the recollection I shut my eyes and tried to shake it from my head. Instead, the memory intensified and expanded. Soon I could see the dark hairs just barely poking through the sweaty skin around his ugly mouth and the long, greasy blond locks that framed his skinny face. Then his scarred and crooked nose came into view, followed by his absurdly prominent jaw that rose and fell cartoonishly with every word. Only, there was nothing funny about him.

"Don't look up," I whispered to myself. "Please don't look up." But I, the me who had lived through that horrible moment, couldn't hear me anymore than I could hear him. I gazed up and into the darkest, meanest black eyes I'd ever seen. They were nothing more than narrow slits of bloodshot coal. The very sight of them made my heart stop and sweat pour from down the sides of my face.

Mercifully, my eyes opened, and instead of staring into the face of a monster, I was sitting by a picturesque stream again, showered in rays of breaking dawn that wove through the gold and orange leaves. I slid down the side of the boulder I'd been perched on, down to the ground, and rested my hot, flushed cheek against the cool stone. My eyes focused on the moving water in front of me, too frightened to remain shut any longer than it took them to blink.

With my eyes open, I couldn't see his hideous face, but that didn't wipe him from my thoughts. As I sat there, with nothing more than the unfamiliar morning songs of strange birds, I racked my brain for a place where the monster fit. *My brother?* No. He looked nothing like me. *A stranger?* No. The passionate hate in his eyes had to be rooted in history. *My husband? Boyfriend?* It was hard to imagine I would ever have fallen in love with that face, but what other relation could have inspired so much fear in my heart?

I was so lost in those thoughts, I didn't hear the sputter of Josh's old truck when he pulled in. I didn't realize I had company until I heard the squish of his boots in the mud and the worry in his voice. "Paige!" he shouted. "Paaaige!"

At the sound of his call, I stopped crying and climbed to my feet. Desperate to see his face, I dropped the knife and ran along the stream to reach him. Forgetting the minor detail that I'd stolen his car and run away, I threw my arms around him and held on as tight as I could. He felt warm, solid, and wonderful.

"Woah!" He threw his arm around my neck and gently embraced me, but at the same time, he took a step back, putting inches of distance between our bodies.

What did you expect? You robbed him.

Then his soft lips pressed a kiss against the side of my head. "Careful," he whispered. "I'm so glad you're okay."

I pulled back and looked him up and down. Confused, I shook my head. "Careful? Are you hurt?"

"No, no." He stroked a small lump where his flannel shirt was messily tucked into his jeans. "I have company." The small mass squirmed beneath the fabric. "What are you doing out here, Paige?"

My damp eyes met his, and my lip trembled. "Where did you go?"

"I got a call," he said. "There was an emergency with a new litter, and I had to leave in a hurry. I didn't want to wake you." He wrinkled his brow. "Didn't you get my note?"

"Note? No. I just heard you run down the stairs, and then you were gone." I frowned and glared at him. "You left me all alone!" I reached out and shoved my hand against his big shoulder, but he barely moved.

His hand caught mine and he pulled it down, held it against his chest. "I left a note on the table saying I would be back in a couple hours."

"A couple hours?! You left me with in the middle of nowhere with no way to call for help if he found me!"

"I'm sorry. I forgot you don't have a phone." He lifted my hand, kissed it, and held it against his stubbly cheek. "I'm so glad you're okay." His gentle touch and sincere eyes pushed all my terror away. "I'll never do it again."

My heart pounded in my chest but not from fear. His hand was strong, and its warmth comforting. The lines of concern on his brow and around his mouth disappeared before my eyes, leaving the scruffy face of a guardian angel. I needed him to hold me, to feel his soft lips. I wanted to climb his towering frame like a tree. Before I could do any of that, however, the lump in his shirt squeaked.

Josh released my hand, opened the button halfway up his shirt, and reached inside. Then he pulled out a tiny bundle of golden fur. As he held it in the palm of his hand, it struggled to lift its little face. With its eyes shut, its mouth opened and a faint cry escaped it.

"Is that—" I squinted for a better view. "Is that a puppy?"

"It is. Daisy, one of my patients, gave birth to a litter the night before last. This little guy has been barely clinging to this world since he came into it."

"He's the smallest puppy I've ever seen."

"He's the runt of the litter." Josh held the sickly baby up, inspected him for a moment, and then gave him a gentle kiss on his head. "He just needs some extra love." He shrugged. "And a whole lot of puppy formula." Josh grinned and flashed his big blue eyes at me. "I was hoping you might help me with that. You know, if you're gonna stick around."

I smiled at the thought of it. *Yes!* My heart jumped at the opportunity to hold him, care for him, and nurse the little baby to health. My head, however, hadn't forgotten the vision of those thin lips and hateful eyes that were somewhere behind me, coming closer every second I wasn't running.

The smile faded from my face. "I can't," I said, my voice little more than a tortured breath.

Then the smile faded from Josh's face too. He nodded, kissed the puppy again, and stuffed it back in his flannel shirt. "Come on," he said. "We have just enough time to get some breakfast and a clean set of clothes before I have to get to the clinic."

My jaw dropped, and I shook my head at him. "Do you ever sleep?"

"Not enough." He took my hand and led me back to

where I'd abandoned the Mustang. Beside it, his rusty blue truck awaited us.

"I'm sorry about your car, Josh. I panicked."

"That's okay." He laughed. "I'm just glad it's not on the wrong side of a guard rail." He tugged my hand playfully. "Who's *he*?"

I looked around at the trees and stream, but we were alone. "Who?"

"You said, 'if *he* found me.' Who is *he*?"

A chill ran right through me.

Josh

We didn't talk much as I led her back to the truck, but I sensed a new calm in Paige, like she had come to terms with something. I still didn't understand what she was so afraid of, but then again, my life was so predictable I really couldn't put myself in her shoes. *How would I feel in a strange place with no idea who I was?*

"Here," I drove with one hand on the steering wheel and pulled the puppy from my shirt with the other. I could feel him squirming and knew it was time to feed him again. "I think he's hungry. There is a bottle in the bag at your feet."

"What?" Paige looked at the wriggling bundle in my outstretched hand like she had never seen anything like it before. "A puppy?" She turned her big eyes on me as I gently deposited the pup in her lap.

"Yes, and he's hungry." One corner of my mouth twitched in a grin. I pulled into Triplets Gas and Groceries. "I'll be right back. I need to pick up some things for breakfast." I rubbed my belly. "I'm hungry too."

I parked in front of a pump, thinking I might as well top the tank off while we were there. Searching for Paige, I had burned through half a tank already that morning. I patted my back pocket, feeling for my wallet as I walked past the pumps and through the front doors of the store. A string of bells chimed to announce my arrival.

The glass cold cases stood at the back of the store, their fronts fogged with condensation. While I would have been perfectly fine with beef jerky and pork rinds for breakfast, I didn't think Paige would feel the same way.

I grabbed a basket from the end of the aisle, and began tossing things in—a bag of coffee, two freckled bananas, some English muffins, a dozen eggs, and a small carton of milk. *That should do it,* I thought, glancing around for anything I might have overlooked. As I walked back to the front, past the candy and junk food aisles, I tossed in a bag of peanut M&Ms, my guilty pleasure.

I was making my way to the register when something new and unusual caught my eye. Triplets Gas and Groceries hadn't offered more than the most basic home essentials in the whole time I'd been stopping there—about thirty years—so the bright green and blue modern display stood out among the paper towels, bread, and quarts of oil. "Wanderfone Prepaid," the sign read. "No Contracts. No Hassles. Unlimited Freedom." I took one of the blister-packed phones down and looked it over.

"...with no way to call for help if he found me!" Paige's words echoed through my mind. "...If he found me!" *HE.*

I flipped the package over and read quickly through the instructions. "Just plug it in, follow the 3-step activation process, and claim your total mobile freedom." The directions were easy enough. I turned it again in my hand. Written across the top, the packaging said, "Works with every major network for universal coverage."

Sold!

On my way to the register, my arms overfilled with convenience store treasures, I caught a glimpse of a familiar blue Stetson with a silver tassel on the brim. He was walking slowly across the parking lot, scanning the vehicles and general area as he approached. "Good afternoon," I said with a smile and a nod as the trooper stepped into the store and let the door shut behind him. The string of bells tied to the door knob jingled.

He nodded back before approaching the counter. "Good afternoon, sir." He waved me by and then followed me to the register. While I unloaded my purchases on the counter, he pulled something from his pocket and held it up to show the cashier. "Would you mind takin' a look at this picture, sir? We're trying to find this woman. Have you seen anyone who looks like her?"

The freckle-faced kid behind the register stared hard at the picture and shook his head. "No, sir. Haven't seen anyone lookin' like that today. Just regulars." He pointed to me. "Like Doc here."

The trooper turned a raised eyebrow to me. "You're a doctor?"

"Veterinarian." I held out my hand, and he shook it. "Josh Dalton. I'm about as close to a doctor as we get around here after tourist season."

He nodded. "Well, you might be especially helpful to this investigation. There was an accident off Shipwreck Road. A pickup went through a guard rail, flipped down a ravine, and landed on its side. Emergency crews are out there pulling it up right now. Funny thing is there was no one in the truck, just a purse behind the driver's seat. But there was blood on the windshield, so the woman driving must have some serious injuries." He squinted at me. "You have a clinic here in town?"

I nodded slowly, trying to maintain a pleasant, curious expression as my stomach turned. "South end of Water Street, the dead end of Quarry Way."

"Has anyone come in seeking treatment for injuries consistent with that sort of accident?" He held the picture up to me. "This woman, maybe?"

My heart pounded in my chest as I looked closely at the enlarged photocopy of a woman's driver's license. Then a mixture of relief and unease flooded through me. I shook my head. “No. I’m sorry.”

“The truck is registered to this woman, and we found her purse under the seat, but given no one’s recognized her, we’re entertaining the possibility that the truck was stolen. We’re waiting for confirmation from the North Dakota state police.”

The face peering back from the black and white photocopy wasn’t Paige. The name on the image said the round, short-haired woman was fifty-year-old Marlene Thomas from Minot, North Dakota. Marlene was five-foot-three and 287 pounds with dark brown hair. Not Paige. *So… is Paige just some serial car theif? Who the hell is the woman in my truck?*

"No, sorry.” I shook my head. “I haven't seen anyone with those kinds of injuries. Did you check Eastern Maine Medical Center?"

"Yes, sir. Nothing yet. It does seem unlikely that someone would have survived that crash and made it all the way to Bangor for treatment. We're waiting to hear back from the North Dakota Highway patrol on the plates."

Beep

His radio went off. "Unit 403," the dispatchers voice crackled, "respond."

He turned his head to the side, toward the radio on his shoulder, and pressed the button. "This is unit 403. Go ahead."

"Truck reported as stolen," the dispatched announced. "Be on the lookout for the driver, now a person of interest."

The trooper squinted, puckered his lips, and nodded. "Roger that." He released the button and turned back to us. "You guys heard that. Have you seen any strangers around?"

The teen shook his head again, "No. A few couples here for gas and passing through, but nothing strange."

"You?" The officer faced me again, pulling up his utility belt and stuffing the paper into his pocket.

"No, sir. I've been busy with a sick pup." I moved up to pay. It was time to get Paige out of there. She had some explaining to do.

I should have just handed over the money, but I couldn't help myself. "Officer?" He turned to me. "What makes you think it was a woman?"

He looked me up and down as if it was a strange question to ask. "Evidence at the scene points to a female occupant."

"What kind of evidence?" The pimply redhead behind the counter grinned perversely as he spared me the awkwardness of appearing too interested.

"An empty coffee cup from a Cumberland Farms gas station. It had red lipstick on the lid."

"How do you know it wasn't a crossdresser?" the kid asked. I raised an eyebrow at him, thankful he was annoying enough to take the cop's attention off me.

"Well, young man," the trooper said, "that crossdresser would have some pretty lips." He winked at the kid and slapped his hand on the counter. "Okay, thanks, guys. Where is your bathroom?"

"Outside, around back." The kid pointed past the coolers and then began to ring me up.

The trooper nodded and pushed back out the doors and walked around the side of the building toward the bathrooms.

"Put the eggs in a separate bag for me, please." The kid's mind was a million miles away. I think the cop had rattled him a bit. Not much exciting usually happened around there, aside from animals deciding to go into labor in the middle of the night.

With my hands full of groceries, I walked quickly back out to the truck and placed them in the bed. I pumped six gallons into the tank, and then climbing back into the cab with Paige.

"He's so cute!" Paige giggled as the little bundle of blonde fur kicked his legs in the air and made little sucking noises while he nursed on the tiny baby bottle she held. I could tell he already had her wrapped around his paw. It was the first time I'd seen her smile, and I'd given her something to smile about.

I smirked along as I watched her. All baby animals are cute, but goldens hold a special place in my heart. Growing up, my first dog was a golden retriever, and if I'd had time, I'd have taken one from Daisy's litter as my own. My life just didn't allow for long walks and games of fetch.

I hated to wreck the mood, but I had to ask. "Did you see the state trooper?"

She sucked in a breath, all smiles gone. "No, was there one here?" She sat up, careful not to jostle the pup. Her head jerked violently as she tried to look everywhere at once.

"Calm down. He's gone. One came in while I was getting groceries. He was asking about you." I bit my lip trying to figure out how to tell her before I gave up and just blurted it out. "They found your truck."

Her face paled. "What did he say?" She leaned back and scrunched down in the seat, so only the top of her blond hair was visible above the bottom of the truck window.

"Just that they're looking for a woman, the owner of the truck. They found a purse under the seat. It belonged to a Marlene Thomas." I narrowed my eyes on her. "That name ring a bell?"

She shook her head. "No, but that doesn't mean anything."

"The patrolman had a picture of the owner. He showed us."

"That's my name? Marlene Thomas?" Her green eyes bored into me, trying to read my mind.

I shook my head. "It wasn't you."

"What? But it was my purse?" She looked startled, eyes wide and lips colorless. The pup had dozed off in her lap, the half empty bottle forgotten.

"No. The truck was stolen in North Dakota. What were you doing in a stolen truck, Paige?"

Chapter Seven

Paige

I stared far into the distance, as though all the answers were just a little farther down the road. "I don't know why I was in North Dakota."

"Is that where you're from?" By his pursed lips and the wrinkles on his forehead, I could tell he was trying hard to remain calm.

I shook my head. "I don't know."

His gaze darted from the road to my face and back again. "You got friends or family there?"

I shrugged and held the puppy close to my chest, more for my comfort than his. "I don't know."

"Does that name trigger anything? Marlene Thomas? Is that your mom, maybe? Is your name Paige Thomas?"

I thought about it for a moment, but none of it rang a bell—not North Dakota or Marlene Thomas… not even Paige. I brought the sleepy ball of fur to my lips and planted the gentlest kiss on his tiny head. "I don't know, Josh."

"Are you running from the cops or—"

"I don't know!" I snapped. "It's bad enough having no

memory! I don't need you constantly reminding me that I don't remember!"

"Well, excuse me," he barked back. "I like you, Paige, and I don't want to find out you're just some pretty car thief on a crime spree."

"I like you, too!" Tears welled up in my eyes and streamed down my cheeks. "And I don't want to find out I'm just some car thief on a crimes spree." I set the puppy on my lap and covered my face with my hands. All the stress, fear, and frustration of the last 36 hours flooded out in a sobs and shudders.

"Paige…" His voice was calm and kind like it had been when I'd first woken up in the clinic. "I'm sorry. Paige—"

"It's okay." I choked on the words, wishing I could say more, not that I had any more to say.

"It's not okay," he whispered. "I'm sorry." I felt his fingers brush across my lap and the weight of the puppy disappeared. When I opened my eyes, I saw him stuffing it back in his shirt. "He's gotta stay warm."

I nodded, but the loss of the pup filled me with even more sorrow. My heart needed something or someone to love so desperately. In the whole world, I knew only Josh and the puppy. The puppy was gone, and Josh was mad at me. I couldn't remember ever feeling so alone.

"I don't think you're a car thief." Josh turned up Seaglass Drive, and the truck rattled as we bounced along the dirt road. "I mean, you *are* a car thief, but I don't think that's *all* you are." He reached across the vinyl bench seat and wrapped his hand around mine. "That fear when you woke up in the clinic—I've never known criminals to be so scared."

I wiped the tears from my face, but they just kept falling. Still, I forced a smile. "You know a lot of criminals?"

He laughed. "No." Slowly, he lifted my hand to his lips and kissed it. "I'm sorry, Paige. The state trooper rattled me." His chest expanded with a deep breath. "*Lying* to the state trooper rattled me. Some of my friends are cops. They're there to protect people in situations like this. I've never been on the wrong side of one before."

"I'd like to say neither have I, but how would I know?" I smiled, this time for real. "You think they can help us?"

"I really do." He pulled into the long driveway to the farmhouse. "They can help you retrace your steps and figure out where this whole mess started. They'd probably figure out who you are by dinner time."

"And then what?"

He came to a stop just outside the front steps and shifted into park. His tired eyes gazed blankly at the house. "Protect you?"

"From what?"

"You tell me." He turned his face to mine, so genuine beneath the dark, handsome exterior. "I bet we'd find out."

I wanted to kiss him. I wanted to apologize for not saying yes to everything he suggested because I knew he was smart and meant so well. I wanted him to know I was sorry for being difficult and complicated. I just wanted to be easy for him, but I couldn't be.

I looked him dead in his lovely blue eyes and frowned with regret. "No. Please don't, Josh." I sniffed and pulled the cuff of my sleeve across my nose. "Take me to a bus station. Help me get a ticket, and I'll go away, and I'll never be your problem again. Just please don't get the police involved."

He winced and looked down at our joined hands. "I'm not gonna drop you off at a bus station. I don't want you to go away." He raised his chin and smiled at me. "You're my challenge. Not my problem."

I grinned back, and a fresh stream of tears flowed down my cheeks.

"I just don't know what to do when someone asks me about you."

I shook my head. "Why would they do that?"

"There's seven hundred thirteen people *exactly* in Whisper

Cove… at least until Chloe gives birth. A new face is gonna stand out."

"Well, tell them…" I thought for a moment. "Tell them that…" I had nothing, but I lifted my chin confidently, anyhow. "I won't let anyone see me."

He laughed, and the motion of his body disturbed the sleepy puppy, who mewled in response and stretched in his flannel cocoon. Josh reached into his shirt and gave it a light stroke from his finger. "Come on." He nodded toward the house. "It's getting too cold out here for him, and I need some eggs and a shower before I head off to work."

I grabbed the plastic bag from the floor of the truck and opened my own door this time. "You want me to cook while you shower?"

He hopped down from the cab, holding the pup securely against him. "You can cook?"

I thought about it for a moment. "I guess so!" An honest, true grin spread across my face. I didn't remember I could cook, I just *knew* I could. That was just as good. "How do you like 'em? Over medium or scrambled?"

"Any way you make 'em," he said.

We came together at the front of the truck and paused. For a moment, we just stared into each other's eyes. I didn't know what to say, but I wished I did. Maybe he didn't know what to say, either, because he put his hand behind my neck, pulled me closer, and placed the sweetest kiss on the top of my head. "It's gonna be okay, Paige."

But I wanted more.

Josh

"Where do you keep the pans?" Paige rattled around the kitchen, opening the oak cupboard doors and banging them shut as she searched through generations of kitchen equipment and utensils. My mom had taken most of her stuff when she and dad moved to town a few years ago, but that still left more gadgets than I'd ever need.

"—Bottom drawer to the left of the stove." Fresh from the shower, I sat on the scarred hardwood floor, drying my hair with an old towel as the pup napped on a blanket beside me. His breathing was strong, and his voice clear as he yipped in his sleep. I couldn't believe how much better he was doing just four hours into regular feedings. Life as the runt of the litter was hard. We weren't his parents, but at least with Paige and me, he had no competition for food.

"Ah hah!" Paige exclaimed. I looked up, struck dumb by the sight of her, bent over, digging in my cupboards, her round ass encased in those form fitting jeans. The vision hit me like a fist to the chest, knocking the breath right out of me. She really was smoking hot.

"Ta-da!" she shouted, coming up triumphant with an old battered egg pan clutched tightly in her right hand. She set the pan on the burner, and grew frustrated as she twisted different knobs and nothing happened.

"Hey, this is weird. How do you work this thing?" She frowned, her forehead wrinkling as she tried to figure out how to light my old gas stove.

"Here." I moved the pup to the box I'd cozied up for him and tossed my wet towel on the chair by the table. Padding over to her in my socks, I noticed peach skin peeking out through a hole in the toe. *Dammit! That looks awful!* I shook my embarrassment off quickly and tried to distract her from the hole with practical instructions. "It's a gas stove. The tank is out back. Twist here," I turned the knob to demonstrate, "and then hold down the igniter."

"Gas?" she cocked her head, holding down the button and listening to the starter click. She turned to me, puzzled.

"We get a lot of snow in winter. Gas means we can cook even when the electricity goes out." I thought about it a moment. "I guess you didn't have a lot of snow wherever you're from."

"I guess not." She still looked confused.

I stood behind her and placed my hand over hers, my body cocooning her for just a second. Taking her hand in mine, I turned the gas to high, and held it there until the flame caught. With the stove turned on, she leaned back into me.

I had to step back. The hands-on lesson lit more than just the stove. Being so close to Paige, smelling my shampoo on her hair, my body reacted with confused feelings I wasn't ready for.

"Hey, Josh!" A knock interrupted my thoughts, and then Mack's voice floated through the kitchen door.

I turned my back on Paige as she cracked eggs into the sizzling pan. As I pulled the kitchen door open, a rush of cool, crisp air rolled over my heated face. The relief was instant, calming the awkwardly eager parts of me.

"Mack! How are you? Come on in." I held it wide, so befuddled I didn't even think about Paige standing at the stove behind me.

"I just couldn't stand it. I had to come see how he was doing. My sweet girl Daisy keeps looking for him—Oh!" Mack stopped dead in his tracks. "I didn't know you had company." He stood just inside the door and gave Paige a quick inspection.

"Uh…" I looked back and forth between them. To my right, Paige stood with the spatula in one hand, eggs sizzling in the pan, and a deer in the headlights look in her eyes. Her golden hair curled around her pretty face, which was flushed from the heat of the stove.

To my left, portly Mack, face ruddy from the chill outside, stood frozen in place, totally baffled. It was like he was shocked to see me in any light than that of the vet, who would come out to his farm at all hours of the night and nurse a runt puppy rather than see it fade away. Like he never expected I would have a life outside of work. Until yesterday, he was right.

"I'm sorry, Josh. I didn't realize you had company." He looked back and forth between us—me with my fresh-from-the-shower hair, Paige barefoot at the stove—and walked right over to her. "Hi, I'm Mack. My wife and I own the hardware store in town." He held out his hand. "You all right?" he asked, sizing up Paige's bruises and then looking at me.

"Oh, she's fine. Just a little fender bender on the way here."

Paige nodded and set the spatula on the counter. She wiped her hand on her pants and offered it to him. "Paige. Nice to meet you, Mack. Have you had breakfast?" She glanced at the eggs, "Oh shit!" Grabbing the handle of the pan and doing something with her wrist, she flipped the eggs in the air without a second thought.

"Paige!" I gaped at her. I'd never seen anyone outside of TV personalities successfully perform that trick.

"Oh, yeah." She laughed. "I guess that was a trick I picked up after college."

"You guys knew each other in college?" Mack was really enjoying this. It was more excitement than our town usually saw in a month.

"Ahhh… yeah," I returned to the pup to hide my discomfort, picking him up from the box and cuddling him. "We met when I was in vet school at Tufts"

"Well, now." He chuckled. "Wait 'til I tell Ma. She'll be so excited to meet your 'old friend' from vet school."

Chapter Eight

Paige

"I'm so sorry, Josh," I said after Mack left. I felt like crying, but my eyes were too dry, and I figured he was sick of the sound of my tears. He was probably sick of my apologies, too.

He stared down at his eggs, his face blank, his eyes shifting as he processed what had happened. "You know, he's gonna tell everyone." He looked up at me and cut his hand through the air. "Like *everyone.*"

I bowed my head and crossed my arms over my waist. "I'm sorry," I whispered.

He shook his head but wouldn't look at me. "It's not your fault. I don't know what the hell I was thinking telling him to come in." He was silent for a moment. "I wasn't thinking.—"

I didn't have anything to say, so I kept my mouth shut and watched him as our eggs grew cold and melted butter turned our toast soggy. My mouth was painfully dry, but I couldn't bring myself to grab my coffee mug.

Then he laughed. "I wasn't thinking. I haven't been thinking since I found you on the side of the road. I've been too busy patching wounds, chasing a runaway, and playing house."

My heart sank. He regretted everything he'd done for me, and there I was, so grateful for his kindness. I trusted him. That morning in the kitchen with the puppy, the way Josh had stood behind me and helped me turn the stove on, even that sweet and simple kiss at the front steps—that was all magical to me. He'd comforted me, made me feel relaxed, safe. He'd even made my heart dream for a moment. But it wasn't real.

There was no place in my life for New England breakfasts, puppies, or love. While I was lost in a fantasy, my situation had turned from bad to worse. I wasn't just the victim of a crash or the prey of an unknown predator; I was a fugitive. Whisper Cove had been the one safe place I'd known in the whole world, and now, I'd lost even that.

"I have to go to work," he said, pushing his chair back from his untouched breakfast.

It was over.

"Can you take me to the bus station on your way?"

Taking his flannel from the back of his chair, he grimaced and put his arms in the dark green and burgundy sleeves. "There are no buses in Whisper Cove after summer. The nearest one is over an hour west in Bangor. I don't have time for that right now." He fastened the black buttons of his shirt. "Besides, I need you to take care of the puppy."

"Me?!"

"You love that puppy. Just keep him warm and fed, talk to him and let him know he's not alone." He walked across the kitchen, pulled something from the white, plastic convenience store bag, and carried it back to the table. He held up a plastic package with a prepaid phone inside. "Nothing's worse than feeling like you're all alone."

I nodded.

"Here." He handed the package to me. "You seem pretty smart. I'm sure you can get that working."

I stared down at the green and blue package and nodded. "For me?"

"I already have one." He pulled his wallet from his back pocket, opened it, and pulled out a small, plain business card. "Don't bother with the office number. It goes straight to the answering service while Chloe's on maternity leave. The after-hours number goes straight to my cell-phone. I'll try to answer that. If I can't, don't leave a message. I'll see the number and call you back as soon as I can."

I stared at the card and read the words out loud. "Whisper Cove Veterinary Clinic, Joshua Dalton, D.V.M."

"That's me." He carried his boots from beside the front door, back to the kitchen table, and sat down to put them on.

My hands were trembling. I was almost afraid to speak and risk ruining whatever was left of our friendship, but I had to. "You don't want me to leave?"

He shook his head. "I don't know what to do, but I know we shouldn't panic. Panic is what flipped you over a guard rail and left you stranded in the middle of the woods this morning. We need a plan." He pulled the cuffs of his pants down over his boots and looked up at me. "Honestly, I don't know what I *want* you to do. I'm more interested in what needs to be done."

On his feet again, he walked over to the box with the blanket and scooped the puppy up with one hand. "Get better, young man," he said firmly. Then he kissed him gently and set him back down on his bed.

Josh came towards me, and I hoped he would kiss me on the head just like he'd kissed the puppy, just like he'd kissed me at the front steps, but he didn't. Instead, he crouched down beside me and stared into my eyes with a deadly seriousness that made my breath stop. "Promise me you won't leave."

I nodded. "I promise."

"If you leave him alone, he'll probably die."

I raised my hand like a scout. "I promise, Josh."

He pursed his lips and looked me over as if to gauge my

trustworthiness. "We need to be smart, Paige. You can't leave without me—there's nowhere for you to go. You're safe here in this house. If you try to leave, you're about 10 miles of hills and woods from civilization. You'll get lost or seen. If the police find you, it's not just *your* neck on the line. I lied to the cops. I lied to Mack. It could cost me everything."

"I promise I won't leave," I told him, my voice stronger, and I meant it.

His big hand took a gentle hold of my chin and raised my face to his. I thought for a moment, hoped, that he would kiss me, but that was foolish. "Smart," he said again. "Smart survives. You understand?"

I understood. There would be no more playing house, no more hugs and kisses on the head. That happiness came at a cost neither one of us could afford. "Yes, I understand."

"Good." He stood up tall again and pointed to the phone in my hands. "Get that working. Call me as soon as it's on. I want to be able to call you if I need you."

If you need me? I didn't ask. "When will you be back?"

"Tonight." He made his way out of the kitchen, through the living room, to the front door. "Barring any unforeseen tragedies." He opened the door, stopped, and looked back at me. "This is gonna be okay, Paige. We're gonna be smart and keep our cool. Everything's gonna be fine… for both of us."

I nodded as he turned and walked out, shutting the door behind him.

Josh was right. We were going to be fine. That was all we would ever be.

Josh

B*ANG! BANG! BANG!*

I looked up to see Avery cupping her hands around her eyes and peering through the glass front door of the clinic.

I closed my eyes for a minute and rolled my shoulders, letting out a deep breath as I tried to work out a little bit of the stress I felt pulling at me.

BANG! BANG! BANG!

She knocked again, waving frantically at me, and I groaned. *Shit!* She'd spotted me. I loved her like a sister, but I was just so tired. This Paige thing had further complicated my already confusing life.

I dropped my pencil on the chart I'd been reviewing and walked around the reception desk to the door, turning the deadbolt with a *snick!*

"Morning, Avery." I walked back and picked up my pencil again, chewing on the end as I waited for her to start in.

"Morning, Josh." She strolled in to my dark waiting room, peering about like she was looking for something. "So," she flipped a lock of hair over her shoulder, "what's this I hear about a girlfriend?" She whirled to face me. Her dark curls bouncing riotously about her face. Artfully applied makeup made her eyes stand out beneath her black lashes and accentuated her cheekbones.

"You talked to Ma," I groaned. "I knew it!"

"Nope, I talked to Caleb, who heard it from Logan. I guess they met for coffee over at the diner this morning." She ticked each step off on her fingers. "Logan heard it from Ma when she was sweeping the front of the store right before she opened. She was most insistent that she had information for the sheriff. I guess she flagged him down when he was walking to meet Caleb."

"And of course, Caleb called you." I sighed and rubbed my temples. Avery was a tall, fiery goddess, and we had been friends for years, but sometimes her personality completely overwhelmed me. I kept hoping she'd fall in love with Caleb so she'd have a designated *someone* to pour all that energy into. Someone who wasn't me. They would have been perfect for each other, but Caleb was a loner, and Avery never seemed to recognize his potential.

“No. He told me while he helped me haul the empties out back for the recycling truck.” She batted her lashes, and her white grin gleamed. “You know I won’t say no to help.”

I chuckled. “Of course not.

“Of course, when we got out back, we had to clean up all the glass.” Her lips turned down in a pouty scowl. “Hooligans smashed every single beer bottle sitting out there waiting for recycling.”

“Again?”

“Again.” She took a deep breath. “But you are trying to distract me. Sooooo?” She tapped a foot as she waited for answers.

“Soooooo… what?” Having a bit of fun, I wondered how long I could drag this out. “Have you talked to Logan about all these problems you are having?”

“Nope.” She leaned on one hip and folded her arms across her chest. “We are not changing the subject. Come on, Josh. Spill! I haven’t seen you with a woman in years. Now you’re shacked up with one? Who is she?” I could see the frustration building in in the lines of her forehead.

“I don't know.” I said, teasing a bit more. I knew that answer wouldn’t work, and sure enough, Avery swung around, hands on her hips, and glared at me. I started to squirm.

“Joshua!”

“Okay, okay!" I took a step back as she advanced and kept my eyes on the floor. "Her name is Paige. We met in college—uh, vet school."

"You? *You* met a girl in vet school? Who is she? How come you never talked about her before? Where has she been? How did you reconnect with her? How long is she in town? What kind of friend is she?" She stalked towards me like a lion after a gazelle, peppering me with questions. She had me in her sights, and I was not going to get away.

"Woah, woah! Slow down. One question at a time." I held up my hands in surrender, backing toward the door. "And not too many. I have a full schedule today—two dewormings and a spay before lunch. I have no help." I moved toward the back hoping she'd relent if she saw me trying to prepare for the day ahead.

"Spill it, Josh!" She followed me, poking around, opening cabinets, and looking at my supplies.

"We… uh… we met in the library. She was… uh… studying…"

"—Don't give me that, Josh. You are full of shit. Don't think I don't see right through you. When do I get to meet your girlfriend, Dr. Dalton?" She whacked me playfully on the arm. All concern gone now that she had peered into my soul and found me entirely unarmed for this battle.

"I… uh—"

"I expect to see you and Paige at the bar at noon. I'll call Logan and Caleb to meet us there. We can all get to know your college girlfriend. It's time you had some help."

Before I could argue, Hurricane Avery was out the door, and Mrs. Preston was pulling Muffy from the car. I glanced down at the schedule, and Muffy was nowhere on it. I had just cleaned that devil dog's teeth a few days ago. *What the hell does she want now?*

Chapter Nine

Paige

I opened my eyes at the sound of tires on gravel coming toward the house. Lifting my head from Josh's pillow, I saw the familiar faded blue pick-up barreling toward me down the drive. I gasped and sat up straight. The clock on the bedside table read 11:33 am.

Something's wrong.

I threw the covers back and jumped out of his bed. An hour was hardly enough to make up for an entire night of lost sleep, but I felt stronger and clearer than when I'd crawled under his blankets. My eyes burned less as I watched him open the truck door and run to the front steps. I quickly pulled my jeans up with a hop, hurrying to see what was the matter.

Grabbing the puppy's box from the other side of the bed, I carried him out to the hall and down the stairs to the living room where Josh was just coming through the door. I was expecting panic or worry on his face, but there was only a light flush from his trot up the steps.

"What's wrong? You said you wouldn't be back until tonight."

Josh smiled, but it was the kind of exaggerated smile you put on to convince a child that everything was okay when everything was absolutely not okay. He took the puppy and the box from my hands. "Nothing's wrong. You took a shower?"

I ran my fingers through my clean hair. "I hope you don't mind. I felt like I needed a fresh start to the day."

"I don't mind." He carried the puppy to the kitchen and set the box down on the floor. Then he turned, stared me up and down, and sighed. "You're beautiful," he said.

My heart fluttered, but my mind refused to be flattered. "Thank you, but I thought I needed to be smart."

"You do." His smile vanished. "*We* do. And right now you have to be an actress."

I shook my head. "What does that mean?"

"This is a small town, and word travels fast. My friends heard about you, and they want to meet you right away."

"Your friends?" I'd spent all my time with Josh alone. It never occurred to me he even *had* friends. "What friends? When?"

"Avery and Caleb and Owen and..." He looked me up and down again. "I'll fill you in on the ride to town. Right now—"

"Ride to town?!" I stood with my eyes wide and my jaw dropped. "I thought you said I had to stay here."

He nodded and held up his hand. "I did, but that was before everyone knew you were here. Now it's more dangerous to keep you hidden."

"More dangerous for *you,* you mean." I couldn't believe it. I hadn't expected Josh to sell me out like that, not after I'd volunteered to leave and never bother him again.

A wounded quiet fell over his face, and he stared at me with hurt eyes. For a moment, he said nothing. I didn't know if I was supposed to apologize, but I didn't. "For *you*," he said. "One way or another, they're going to see you. If you don't go there and meet them like it's no big deal, they'll come looking for you... and then it *will* be a big deal, Paige."

My eyes closed, and my hand cradled my forehead. "So now your friends are after me too?"

"They are not *after* you. They're just protective of me." He stepped toward me and set his big hands on my shoulders, sending tingles all through me. "I told them I met you at vet school. Most of us grew up here and then went to the University of Maine together, but we went our separate ways after that."

"Where did you go to vet school?" I asked. *How the hell am I going to pull this off?*

"Tufts."

I shook my head. "Where the hell is Tufts?"

"Massachusetts."

"Tufts in Massachusetts. You want me to pretend I'm a veterinarian from Tufts in Massachusetts." I gaped at him in total disbelief as he nodded. "And when they see right through that, what do you plan to tell them?"

Josh's strong arms pulled me toward him, and he kissed me on the forehead. I would have enjoyed that if it hadn't been to silence me. "Just nod and turn the conversation back to things you know."

"I don't know *anything*, Josh." I pushed him away looked up to find him biting his lip. "This is a disaster!"

Without a trace of humor on his face, he nodded. "That's okay. These are the people you want with you in a disaster."

While I stood there, unsure what to say, he took a step back and looked at my clothes. "You can't wear that t-shirt. It looks like you've slept in it."

"I have. Twice."

"Upstairs, in the guest room you slept in, the closet is still full of my mother's old clothes. Her nicer things. She's about the same size as you. Can you go find something fresh to wear?"

"Fresh?" I laughed. "From your mother's old closet?"

He nodded, failing to recognize the lunacy of it all. From the look on his face, I could tell there was no arguing with him. Anyhow, if he was right and they were determined to see me, it was better I went to them than for them to come looking for me.

Leaving him in the kitchen to give the puppy his noon feeding, I dragged my feet up the stairs to the guest room and opened the closet door. I pulled a chain hanging from the center of the dark space, and light beamed out from a naked bulb. The closet, more like a small room, was filled from front to back with countless pieces of a prized wardrobe, each individually protected in garment bags. Whoever his mother was, there was no doubt she took fashion very seriously.

I flipped through the hangers, trying to ignore the creepy knowledge that I was picking through another woman's things. I had no idea why she'd left or how old she'd been when she'd bought the clothes. Maybe she'd acquired them over the course of a lifetime. I didn't have time ponder her style or admire her collection. I just needed something to wear.

The first shirt I came to, something white beneath thin plastic, I pulled down and laid out on the bed. I took Josh's tired t-shirt off and let it drop to the floor. Then carefully, as I knew she must have, I pulled the plastic bag over the hanger and stood in awe.

The white linen blouse was beautiful. Pleats swooped down from a collar lined with short ruffles that ran the whole length from breast to waist. The arms were light and billowy, ending with another modest ruffle around the fitted cuffs. The neckline was low enough to be feminine, but high enough to remain classy. With care, I removed the hanger and slipped my arms inside. It was as if it had been made for me.

As I closed the mother-of-pearl buttons, I decided to leave the top two open so I wouldn't look too innocent. I wanted to impress his friends, but I also wanted Josh to notice me.

Tucking the loose hem into my jeans, I admired myself in the mirror. All I needed was a belt. Fortunately, Mrs. Dalton had collected plenty of those.

When I finally made my way down the stairs, Josh was standing by the door, waiting for me. He grinned. "Wow I never saw Mom in that one."

"Do I look okay?"

"No," he whispered. Then he cleared his throat. "You look like an angel."

Josh

Flying down the road toward town, I kept an eye on my watch as I listened to her stumble through the story. We had about fifteen minutes before we met the gang for lunch, fifteen minutes to memorize a lost love affair that never happened between two people who barely knew each other in a place she'd never been. I clenched my jaw, forcing occasional glances at the puppy on her lap to calm myself down. "That's not it," I said, shaking my head.

She groaned and stared out the window. "You told me Tufts!"

"Yes, I did, but—"

"You said Tufts and vet school!"

"No, Tufts *was* vet school. There was nothing after Tufts."

The puppy squeaked and repositioned himself on her thighs.

"Okay. So we met freshman year at Tufts?"

"No—" I stopped myself and took a breath. "Freshman year was at UMaine. That came before Tufts."

"Okay." She swallowed and began again. "We met our freshman year at UMaine—"

"No, Paige. We met at Tufts." Feeling the need for something soft and soothing, I reached across the front seat and scooped the puppy from her lap. I set him gently on my own and stroked his soft, golden fur. He lifted his head, looked back at Paige and whimpered. "They all went to UMaine. They'll know you weren't there."

She threw her hands in the air like she was tossing the pieces of an impossible jigsaw puzzle. "I give up! I told you this was a horrible idea. They're gonna know we're making it all up."

I turned onto Shipwreck Road, the main artery leading in and out of Whisper Cove, and shook my head. "Not if we don't make it all up." I could see her turn her head to me from the corner of my eye, and I glanced over to catch her narrow gaze.

"What do you mean?" Her voice was hard with worry.

"I mean…" I petted the puppy in my lap again as I pulled my thoughts together. How could I convince her to trust people she'd never met when she believed her very life depended remaining hidden? "I mean they're going to find out one way or another, Paige. If we don't tell the truth, they'll know."

"Then turn around and take me back to the house." Her voice rose with panic. "We don't have to meet them at all, Josh. We don't have to say *anything!*"

"Avery will never let it go. I told you—if we don't come to her, she'll come to us."

"Then take me to the bus station in Bangor, and I'll leave. *Avery*—" she sneered as she said the name, "—doesn't have to worry about some liar shacking up with you."

"Calm down, Paige." She was panting and red-faced. I would have pulled over to give her a moment to get herself together, but I was afraid she'd jump out of the truck, run into the woods, and disappeared forever. She was a pain, a time-consuming complication, and I didn't know why exactly, but I didn't want to lose her.

She gasped in a huge breath and folded her arms across chest. "*You* calm down."

"I'm calm," I told her, dragging my fingers along the worried puppy's back. "You're scaring him."

She looked down at the pup and a frown spread on half her face. "I'm sorry." Then she shifted her gaze up to me. Her eyebrows came together as she wrinkled her nose. "Why *are* you so calm?"

I flashed an easy smile at her. "Because I know these guys. I've known them a long time."

She studied my face. "You trust them."

I nodded.

"Well, I don't know them." She stared down the long, winding road ahead. "And I don't trust them."

I reached across the empty space between us, took her hand in mine, and gave it a squeeze. As kindly as I could, I reminded her, "You don't know *anyone*. You don't trust *anyone*."

She turned her eyes down to our joined hands and gave a weak squeeze back. "I trust you." She blinked up at me, her eyes damp, but not yet teary.

"Then trust me, Paige. *Really* trust me. If you have any chance of surviving this whole thing—the wreck and whatever trouble you're in—you're gonna need help. I can patch you up and share with you everything I have, but…"

"But?"

I sighed, hating to admit I couldn't be everything she needed. "I can't help you solve this mystery… not like Caleb can. And I can't protect you like Logan can. That's not how we work. We're a team. We all bring something to the table, Paige. That's how friends work. That's how this whole town works. They would never hurt you." I stopped for a moment and thought about that. Then I brought her hand to my lips and kissed her delicate fingers. "*I* would never hurt you."

She didn't smile or cry. She just looked at me for what seemed like a very long time. Then she nodded. "I do really trust you. If you trust them, I will too."

"Really?!" A wide smile spread across my face, and my heart throbbed in my chest. "This really is the right decision. You'll see."

"Really." She took the puppy back from my lap, pressed her lips against his head, and then set him down on her thighs. You couldn't stay upset, not with a puppy in your life. "I'm just scared," she whispered.

"—I know you are, but that's mostly because we know nothing about you. They can help us. Have you remembered anything?" Her confidence in me, and now my friends, made me even more determined to figure out who Paige was and what she was running from.

"No." She shook her head and her golden hair cascaded over her shoulders. "Nothing." I nodded, but I knew she was lying to me. She *had* remembered something. I could see it in her eyes, in the way she looked out the window when she answered me. But I didn't have time to press her about it.

I reached for her hand, wrapping mine around it, feeling how icy her fingers were. "You need this, Paige. As much as I love having you, you can't hide in my house forever. That's no life for you. Give these guys a chance. You'll like them, I promise. Well, you'll like Caleb and Logan, anyway. Avery can take a while to grow on you."

"Why do you always talk like that about her?"

I thought about it for a moment. "She's… pushy. She has to be to run a bar alone. She's just… a very strong individual... but she is loyal as hell."

"That's who came to your clinic?" With one hand still stroking the puppy, the other she gripped tighter around mine.

I stroked the back of her hand with my thumb and slowed

the truck as we approached the city limits. "Yes. We've been friends for years. She saw right through me, when I lied about you in my office. She's gonna have questions. Prepare yourself."

She flicked her eyes up at me. “Friends?”

“No,” I chuckled, “not *that* kind of friends.”

She smiled and looked away. "Josh?”

“Yeah?”

“I'm afraid of what they might find."

“I know.”

Her tired stare focused ahead at the cars gathered around Whisper Cove's only traffic light. Dark circles ringed her eyes, and I remembered hearing her crying in her sleep the night before. At least, I'd thought she was asleep.

I gave her hand a little wiggle. “You okay?”

She yawned. "Tell me more about them."

“My friends?” She nodded. “Well, Caleb and Logan will be there. Owen and Dan will probably be busy." I mentally ran through my conversation with Avery. “It shouldn't be more than the five of us. The rest of my friends will trickle in tonight. We all usually gather at the bar and play softball after work.”

She raised her eyebrows. “You play softball at the bar?”

“Well, out back. Logan and the Mayor talked Avery into letting them convert the empty lot into a field.”

“The Mayor?”

I shook my head and laughed. “That's Owen. I'm sorry. We've been calling him that so long, I almost forget it's not his real name.”

“But he won't be there?”

“Not for lunch. Caleb will, but he won't say much. He's quiet. Ex-military. He got hurt pretty bad in the war.”

“Is he a…” She looked at the dash as she struggled for the word. “A… a jarhead? Is that what they call them?”

“Yup. They do, and he is. But he's a pussy cat. You'll

notice one side of his face is scarred. He had a run-in with an IED. He doesn't talk about the incident… or the war. He lost a lot of friends."

"Oh no, that's awful."

"Everyone's got a story." I grinned and gave her hand one final squeeze before pulling mine away to take a sharp right onto Water Street. "He's a good guy, though. And he does this thing with computers… he can find anything or anybody. We need him on our side."

"And Logan... he's the sheriff?" Her question ended in a squeak, betraying her fear about the upcoming meeting.

"Yeah. Logan and I met in kindergarten. He's a little straight-laced and stuffy, but all around a good guy."

"But he's the sheriff. Won't he turn me in?"

"Turn you in to whom?" I rolled my eyes and offered her a crooked smile. "I keep telling you. This is Whisper Cove, Paige. We take care of our own. You're important to me, so you'll be important to them." I pulled into the parking lot outside of Avery's bar. Caleb's SUV sat in the same spot he always picked, right outside the window where he liked to sit.

"Are you sure?" She looked up at me one more time, tears filling her eyes and threatening to spill over.

"I'm positive. Now cuddle that puppy. He can't get cold. And come on in. It's time to face the music."

I walked around to the other side of the truck and opened the door to help her out. Stretching my arm around her, I kept her close as we walked into Avery's.

"Hey, Josh! Over here!" Logan called from the booth in the corner. As usual, Caleb sat in the shadows with his scarred side facing the wall and a ball cap pulled low over his eyes.

"Come on." I steered her around the tall, mostly empty tables. Smiling, I tipped my head at the few regulars.

"Logan. Caleb." I nodded, and they both stood to greet Paige, who was trying to make herself shrink away. At five-foot-eight, almost as tall as Avery, that was no small feat.

"Hey, Josh, I've got a Shipyard for you." Avery appeared almost instantly with a cold bottle of beer and a chilled glass on a tray. She set it on the table in front of me and stuck the tray under one arm. Holding her hand out to Paige, she said, "Hi, I'm Avery."

Surprised by Avery's bold greeting, Paige shifted the puppy from one arm to the other and offered her own hand in return. "I'm Paige. It's nice to meet you."

Avery's blue eyes sparkled. "A pleasure. What will you have?" She waited with her red lips turned up in an enormous smile.

Paige, looking startled and a little bit frightened, turned to me. I took a step closer to her, and smiled back at Avery. "Maybe just grab her a bottle of water for now. Let's give her a minute to decide. I'm sure one of your fabulous craft beers will catch her eye. You got menus somewhere?"

"Yeah, give me a minute. I stuck them ah… over there." Avery made her way back to the bar and grabbed a couple menus and a bottle of water as I ushered Paige into the booth between me and Logan. It was kind of unfair, but I was a little afraid she might bolt if she wasn't trapped.

"So..." Logan looked from me to Paige. "You two met in college?" He raised a skeptical eyebrow.

Paige and I exchanged glances. Just like I'd warned her, my friends weren't buying it. To spare her the discomfort of explaining, I took over. "That's kind of a story." I placed a hand on Paige's knee under the table to reassure her.

"A story, huh?" Caleb's low rumble rolled across the table. He spoke so rarely I had almost forgotten he was there. He watched Paige from under the bill of his hat. "I love stories."

"Uh... well. I…" She stammered and turned to me for rescue.

"Here's the thing, guys." I leaned toward the center of the table, and they leaned closer in return. "We need your help."

"Help?" Logan's eyes narrowed, and he looked Paige up and down. "What kind of help?"

"Well, I kinda found Paige on the side of the road." I shook my head. "We don't know who she really is."

"See! I told you!" Avery appeared suddenly at the end of the table and jabbed a finger at Logan. "I told you he wasn't telling me everything!"

"Wait a minute," Logan said, holding a hand out to quiet Avery. He looked at me. "You don't know who she is?" Then he turned to Paige. "You don't know who you are?"

"I, um…" She fumbled her words, her face turning red.

"It's okay, Paige." I moved my hand from her knee and placed it on her fingers as they trembled atop the table. "She hit her head. She has amnesia. Dial it back a bit, okay guys?"

"You were the driver of that truck that went off the road up on the cliff?" Avery stood there putting the pieces together, and handed Paige her water. "You survived that?" She glanced out front to where Tommy's tow truck sat in front of the diner. Paige's mangled escape vehicle lay in a crumpled heap strapped to the flatbed.

Paige wordlessly nodded, glancing over at me.

"Yeah." I looked up at Avery as the disturbing memories of blood and glass and twisted steel flashed across my mind. "I found her and got her out before it fell all the way. Had to rappel down about twenty feet."

"Shit, man. I saw that scene." Logan's eyes widened as he looked at Paige. "You were lucky he got you out of there. The fall to the bottom would have killed you."

"Three hundred forty-seven feet," Caleb announced. Paige's eyes widened. We were used to his random recitation of facts, but she wasn't. Caleb's mind worked a little differently than the rest of us. He was freaking brilliant, and he remembered everything. It's what made him so good at what he did. It's why Paige needed him so badly. We both did.

"A long way," Logan agreed. "Tell me, what do you remember about the accident?"

"I don't remember anything." Paige shrunk between her shoulders and leaned away from Logan and into my side.

Logan looked up from her to me. "Why didn't you come to me before this? You know that truck was stolen?" He dropped a suspicious gaze to Paige. "Did you steal that truck?"

"I… I don't remember." Her voice was weak and terrified. "I'm sorry. I don't know."

"It's not that simple, Logan." I looked down at my hand and Paige's. "She's scared of something or someone."

He nodded. "Yeah… someone like the police?"

I locked eyes with my old friend and shook my head. "Logan, we need your help. We need to figure out who she is and where she's from. We need to figure out who's after her, and we need to figure it out fast." I wrapped an arm around Paige's shoulders. "We need to find them before they find her."

Across the table, Caleb nodded. "I'm in."

"I'm in too," Avery said.

"Thank you." I sent a hard glare at Logan and then turned my attention to the volunteers. "Caleb, I need your computer magic." I reached into my back pocket and pulled out a receipt. "This is all she had on her when I pulled her from the wreck. They found a purse in the truck, but I hadn't seen it in the dark. It fell so fast I barely got her out."

"It's not her purse," Logan said. "It was stol—"

"—stolen," I said, cutting him off. "Thanks for the news-flash, Sheriff Fox. Is Logan around? I could really use his help. My friend's in trouble. She ran once already. I found her in the woods clutching the biggest knife she could find from my kitchen." I glared as hard and dark as I could. "Someone. is. after. her."

Logan pursed his lips and looked past Paige to me. "Can we talk for a minute? You and me?"

I pulled her close, and she leaned against me, practically climbing into my skin to get away from him. "We can talk right here," I told him. "She risked everything by coming here and being honest with you guys. She deserves the same in return."

Logan's nostrils flared as he sharpened his eyes on me. He took the gas receipt from the table, opened it, and looked it over. He thought for a moment and then looked up at Paige. "If I find out you're lying…"

She pulled away from me, sat up straight, and lifted her chin to him. "I may be wrong, but I'm not lying."

He nodded. "All right." He held the receipt between his fingers and looked at me. "I can keep this?"

"Yeah."

He folded it and tucked it in his shirt. "I'll make some calls."

"Thank you. And Avery," I turned to her, "you see everyone. You know everyone. They all tell you things. I need your ears to keep her safe. Can you do that? Please?"

Avery came to stand in front of me, and she looked deep into my eyes. "You know I'll always help you, Josh." Then she reached past me, took Paige's hands in hers, and smiled kindly. "How can I help *you*, darlin?"

Chapter Ten

Paige

After lunch, there wasn't enough time for Josh to drive me home before he had to be back at the clinic, so I spent the afternoon in his office with the puppy. Avery had offered to take me up to her place so I could borrow some things, but there was something about her that made me uncomfortable. She was sweet and friendly, but almost too familiar to be a total stranger. I thanked her for the offer but kept as close to Josh as I could.

That wasn't purely out of fear.

I liked Josh. From the time he first drove me back to his house, I found something in him I could relate to. He wasn't just tall, strong, and handsome. He wasn't just my rescuer. More than just the dashing doctor who kept all the female pet-owners of Whisper Cove coming around, Josh was flawed and desperate… just like me.

I watched him move from exam room to exam room, overworked and exhausted, and I wanted to give him rest. When he stared at charts, his forehead wrinkled with worry about illnesses he couldn't cure, I wanted to ease his mind. At the end of the day, when the last wounded animal and needy owner had walked out the door, I wanted to dress Josh's wounds and tend to his needs.

All I thought of on the way home that night was how amazing he was and how much I wanted to amaze him in return. He'd taken me into his clinic, into his home, into his circle of friends. He'd shared himself with me when I had no one else in the world, and I wanted to share myself with him. But honestly, what I wanted more than anything was to be even closer to him.

On the ride home, I slid across the bench seat of the old truck, wrapped his arm around my shoulders, and rested my head against him. He gave me one of those sweet, innocent kisses on the head, the one I'd craved so much earlier, and it made my heart flutter. But it wasn't enough.

Somehow, in the short time I'd known him, I'd moved past my fear. I didn't want to run anymore. I didn't need a kiss on the head to let me know that everything would be all right. I needed *him*.

When we reached the house and he opened my door for me, my hand didn't tremble in his as he helped me down. I didn't turn away when he looked into my eyes. With the pup cradled in my arms, I held his gaze all the way to the front door.

Inside, I walked straight to the kitchen and laid the sleeping puppy in his cardboard bassinet. Josh set his leather bag on the table and looked around. "You want some frozen lasagna? We could try the eggs again. I don't think I ate any of—"

Before he could say another word, I reached up over his broad shoulders, and wrapped my hands around the back of his thick neck. I pulled his face down to mine, stretched up on the tips of my toes, and pressed my lips against his. Hanging like an ornament from his massive frame, I waited for him to respond, to kiss me back or push me away. For what seemed like an eternity, he did nothing.

Suddenly ashamed of my misguided forwardness, I flattened my feet, released my hold on his neck, and broke our kiss. I took a step back and began to turn so he wouldn't see embarrassment on my face. *You fool. Of course he doesn't want—*

Before I could sink into that darkness, his hands were on my hips, turning me back to him. His lips met mine with such a ravenous hunger I almost didn't notice my feet leaving the floor until I was laid out on the kitchen table. I felt my head whipping back and closed my eyes to prepare for impact, but the back of my skull landed cradled in the pillow of his palm. A moment later, he pulled away from our kiss and my body, and stood tall between my dangling legs.

His sky blue eyes locked on mine as we both gasped to catch our breath. His gaze wandered up and down my body. Then he reached down and pulled his white t-shirt up over his head, exposing a bare chest that could have been sculpted by a renaissance master. His pecs and abs heaved with every excited breath. He let his shirt drop to the floor and licked his lips while he studied the curves of my breasts through my linen shirt.

I started to sit up, reaching for his body, but he gently forced me back down. His fingers worked their ways to gaps between my buttons, and with one dramatic *ripppp* he tore the lovely blouse open, launching mother of pearl buttons in all directions. Frustrated by the distance my lacy bra put between us, he reached down with both hands and tore it in two just over my heart.

Lying there, my body exposed, the object of my desperate desire beyond my reach, I moved to sit up again.

"Stay down." He swallowed as he drank in the sight of my naked chest and hard nipples. Bending over, he opened his mouth between my breasts and began a series of kisses, licks, and love bites that extended all the way down my navel. At the same time, his skillful fingers unbelted me, unbuttoned my jeans, and dragged my zipper down. He gripped both sides of my pants and panties and easily lifted my bottom off the table to slide my clothes down, exposing my thighs and mound to him.

Like we'd rehearsed this dance, he lowered his face between my thighs, and my fingers combed through his hair, pressing him further down. I felt the soft, wet drag of his tongue along my seam, the sensations so hot, traveling so fast from his lips to my brain, I cried out in anticipation as I waited for him to taste my clit. I could almost feel his mouth smiling against my plush lips as he made me wait in agony for more. Then, when I was almost pleading, he parted my legs, exposing my eager, throbbing clit to the cool air, and latched on to me.

His tongue danced the lightest circles around my bud, his performance designed to leave me wanting more, and I did. I *needed* more.

"Josh." I moaned his name like a prayer.

"Mmmm," he mumbled back, never taking his mouth from my pussy.

"I want you inside me."

Suddenly he stopped everything. I lay there, waiting for him to stand, unzip himself, and slide inside me, but he didn't. He simply pulled his face from my lap for a moment and said, "No."

I gasped. I had no idea what to say or do. No man had ever refused me before. At least, I had the feeling they never had. While I lay there, hot, hungry, clumsily trying to gather my wits, he dove down again, latched on, and his dance continued.

With nothing to do but lie there and enjoy it, I grabbed hold of the back of his head and began to rock against his tongue, riding his face as the ecstasy grew more and more intense. I could feel a pull inside me, like gravity on the crest of a hill. I knew I was about to go over the top and ride it all the way to the bottom.

I pushed his head down harder between my legs and lifted my hips higher. "Oh my God, Josh! Don't stop! I'm gonna come!" But that's exactly what he did.

His big hands pulled my wrists away from his head and he lifted his face, leaving me there, dripping on the kitchen table. I opened my eyes just in time to see him reaching down around my hips. Without a word, he hoisted me off the table and held me against him. I wrapped my legs around his waist and buried my mouth in his kiss.

I could taste myself on his lips and in his stubble, and it only made me want him more. I showered him in licks and kisses as he carried me into the living room and lowered me onto the braided rug. He stood above me and finally slid his light blue scrubs and boxers down in one motion, revealing his cock to me for the first time.

I don't know if I'd ever seen a bigger one, or any other cock at all, but it seemed massive in the dim light. It was long and thick, and beautiful. I dropped to my knees before him, and without thinking, guided its gorgeous mushroom head into my mouth.

Without a memory, my tongue moved by intuition, rolling in slow, wet circles around the rim, and painted sloppy laps all over the head. Josh drew a deep breath through his teeth. I stayed there for a while, worshiping him and the tip of his massive member with my lips before opening wide and taking in as much of his shaft as I could.

I took him in until his cock reached the back of my throat, making me gag gently. I could hear him groan over me, and I liked the sound, so I did it again, impaling my throat with him. Finally, the third time, he could wait no longer. He pulled his prick from my mouth and pushed me back onto the rug.

Climbing between my legs, his sparkling blue eyes stared deep into mine.

"You're mine," he whispered. "I'll keep you safe forever."

He didn't wait for a response before he slid the throbbing head of his hard member between my lips, found my entrance, and pushed into me like he was coming home. He buried himself as far as my body would let him and stopped when a tiny yelp escaped me. My legs opened and wrapped around his waist as he drove his shaft into me again and again. My every groan he met with a deep, animal grumble which only made my body need him more.

As the heat rose, and I came again to the peak of that mountain, I threw my head back, arched my spine, and prepared to ride him right over the top. He wrapped his arms beneath the small of my back, lifted me up higher, and caught one hard, tender nipple between his teeth. He held it there, biting just hard enough to make me cry in pleasure and beg for more.

I was afraid to tell him I was going to come again, afraid he'd pull out and leave me desperately wanting more, but I couldn't help myself. "Yes, please! God! Josh!"

And then I was melting in his arms, convulsing with pleasure as he exploded deep inside me.

Josh

Flat on my back, I traced the cracks in the ceiling with my eyes. Paige snuggled in the crook of one arm, letting out the cutest, softest snores. I think it was the first real sleep she's had since I'd pulled her from the wreck.

My brain still high on endorphins, I enjoyed the sounds and smells of the old house around me. The creak in the floors, the wind making the tree branches scrape against the wood siding, the shelves filled with dusty books piled high to the ceiling—these familiar surrounding made me think of all the Dalton men who'd come before me and lay there on that same rug with a beautiful woman sleeping contented in their arms.

"Mmmmh," she stretched and rolled on her side, throwing a leg over mine as she stayed close in the protective shelter of my arms. Her eyelids fluttered open. "That was… unexpected."

I raised an eyebrow. "Pretty sure that was more than unexpected. That was amazing."

"Yeah," she purred like a cat, "it was, wasn't it?" Her delicate fingers played in the springy hair on my chest, pulling the curls out and watching them snap back.

I yawned. The last several crazy days of relentless emergencies was catching up with me.

"Josh?" My name came out as a question, making me look down at her blonde waves that spread across my arm.

"Yes, sweetheart?"

"I need to tell you something."

"Okay," I shifted so I could see her.

She raised her long lashes, her soft green eyes looking straight into mine. "I remembered something."

"You did?" I scrambled back, pushing up into a seated position, my back against the couch.

She rolled over onto her stomach and lifted herself off the floor, coming to sit in front of me. "When I ran, when I was alone by the creek, I saw a man."

"In the woods? There was a man there? Why didn't you tell me?"

She smacked my foot, "No, let me finish. I *remembered* a man. His face. He… I was scared of him." She sat there, a blonde goddess, sunset through the windows casting a pink glow around her.

"Who was he?" I asked tentatively. This was the first time

she had really opened up to me, and I didn't want to mess it up.

"I don't know. I just remembered his face, and he was saying something. I couldn't make out the words, but he..." she shivered.

I reached out and pulled her to me, tugging another of my grandmother's quilts off the arm of the high-backed chair and wrapping the soft fabric around us. The random shapes and colors of the crazy quilt made a fitting representation of our mixed up lives.

"You saw a man, a brother?"

"No," she shook her blonde curls. "He wasn't family."

"A husband? Boyfriend?"

"Maybe." she seemed unsure, but she hadn't said no. "I'm not wearing a ring. I think I would know if I was married. There's not even a tan line." She held up her hand, and I could see in the dusk light that she was right. No ring. No tan line. Not even a dent in the flesh. In fact, when I found her she hadn't worn any jewelry at all except for simple studs in her ears.

I leaned over and snagged the leg of my pants, pulling the pile of clothes over and digging in the right pocket.

"What are you doing?"

"Calling Caleb."

She pushed back from me. "Why?"

"He needs to know this. Hang on. He may have some questions."

I pressed a few buttons, pulled up my favorites list, and scrolling down to Caleb's name. I pressed 'send' and the phone rang twice before Caleb's voice came over the line. "Caleb here."

I put the call on speaker so she could hear too. "Hey, it's Josh. I'm here with Paige, and she just remembered something."

"Hey Josh. Hang on. Let me grab a notebook." We heard scrambling background noise for a moment. "Okay, go."

I ran my hand down her back and pulled her into my embrace. "Tell him what you told me."

She nodded. "I… um… I saw a face. A man. He was angry, yelling. He was after me. I could just feel it." She shivered in my arms, and I pulled the quilt up over her shoulders.

"What did he look like? Tell me everything you remember. No detail is too small."

"Um… he had squinty coal black eyes and thin lips." She gestured around her face. "He had a dark stubble, and longish dirty blonde hair. Um… not just dirty-blond, but really dirty, greasy. Bad skin—lots of acne scars. A crooked nose like it had been broken and never set right."

"Hmmm, okay. I'm going to run a search through missing persons for you. I'll see what pops up in the North Dakota law enforcement database."

"You have access to that?" she looked at me, eyes wide, startled.

Dead silence came over the line.

"Ah, no babe, Caleb has… methods. I told you he was good. He's got some secret supercomputer in his basement. We just don't ask."

"It's not that cloak and dagger," he said. "But anyway, I'm also going to search the database for any missing persons who match your description. Did he have any identifying features? Scars? Tattoos?"

She shook her head, even though Caleb couldn't see her. "No… at least not in my memory."

"Tattoos possible." I could hear the scratch of his pen on paper. "Okay, then."

"Thanks, Caleb. Let us know if you find anything."

"Night, Josh. Bye, Paige."

Click

I tightened my arms gently around her. "If you're on the

run from a boyfriend, there has to be a reason. He doesn't sound like a nice guy." I didn't even know if he existed, but I was already talking shit about him.

She shook her head. "He doesn't feel like a nice guy."

"Somebody, somewhere is missing you, Paige. Someone good. Family. Friends." I kissed her head. "Caleb will find them."

Chapter Eleven

Paige

Dawn's first light broke over the red and orange leaves, filtered through the panes of glass, and landed in a faint window-shaped pattern on the quilt Josh and I snuggled under. I'd been awake for a while by then, quietly watching the sky turn from black to deep cornflower blue and now lavender with bright pink rising up from the distant horizon. A thin blanket of frost covered the grass and truck and made me appreciate even more the warmth of his strong chest beneath my cheek.

For the moment, his breathing was slow and regular, the pattern of a deep, restful sleep, but I knew it couldn't last. The world would grow brighter. Josh would wake to a headful of responsibilities and dutifully leave our embrace to fulfill them. I'd rise with him to face my own to-do list but with less enthusiasm. At the top of that list, well, right under puppy duties, was Avery.

It wasn't that I didn't like her. In fact, of all the people I currently knew in my life, she was second only to Josh. She was kind and friendly. Her manner was bold, which meant I didn't have to be. She talked, and I could just listen. Her natural charisma made up for so much of my awkwardness it was easy to be with her. She was the perfect friend, only… her face. Every time I looked at her, it was like seeing a ghost. I almost remembered, but could never quite make a connection.

I felt Josh's chest rise high with a deep breath and fall with a gentle groan. Then his arms wrapped around me, and he planted a kiss on my forehead. "You awake, angel?"

I smiled and turned my lips up to meet his for a quick kiss, but when our lips met, I could feel the heat rising inside me, and I couldn't pull away. His mouth opened, and mine did too as my hand reached down to find his shaft already stiff and growing harder in my grasp. His strong hand landed on the curve of my hip, and he rolled me on my back, positioning himself between my open thighs. His soft lips descended on my hard nipple, but before we could really start, duty called.

Ruh-ruh-ruh-ruuh-reer-reeer-reeeeeeer!

Josh dropped his head and rested his stubbly cheek on the soft skin between my breasts. He wrapped his arms around the small of my back and sighed. "Puppies."

I sighed too and stroked his hair. "Puppies," I whispered.

"He needs a name."

"Mack didn't give him one?"

He shook his head. "No. He thinks it's bad luck to name a sick newborn."

"What?" I turned my head to the puppy's cardboard box on the floor and frowned. "That seems… heartless."

"Not heartless. Just thinking about the wrong heart. A lot of people think like that." He lifted his head, planted a kiss where his face had been, and smiled up at me. "Come on. Let's get this show on the road."

While I showered, he made breakfast. When I made my way to the kitchen there were two plates of eggs, toast, and bacon sitting on the kitchen table. Josh was sitting on the floor, smiling down at the puppy, who eagerly sucked at a tiny rubber nipple on the bottle of formula Josh held for him. When he heard me enter, he looked up and shared that smile with me.

"You look beautiful," he said.

I stared down at myself in the blue, form-fitting, long-sleeved shirt and matching pleated skirt. "You think so?" I hadn't felt very confident about it when I'd pulled it from his mother's closet, but my options were limited. My only pair of underwear was dirty, and I wasn't about to go around town commando in his mom's jeans. All her other dresses were light and sleeveless. "Everything else seemed kind of summery."

He nodded. "Mom's a snowbird. She keeps her winter clothes in Florida." With the puppy losing interest in the bottle, Josh rose to his feet and held him out to me. "Here. Rub him gently like you're his mother licking him. It will help his digestion."

"Okay." I took the puppy and sat at the table. As Josh poured us some coffee, I stroked the baby's soft fur. He was growing bigger, heavier already. "Have you thought of a name?"

"Me?" He set the coffee on the table and fetched the cream and sugar. "I figured that could be your job."

"Mine?" A happy little grin budded on my lips. "Why me?"

Josh sat down across from me. "You seem to be his favorite."

"He likes you too."

"Not as much as you." Josh reached over to take the puppy from my hands, and as soon as he did, the puppy began to cry. "See? You two have a thing."

I smiled and held the puppy up to look in his little golden face. "You look like... a... Jentil."

Josh laughed. "Gentle? With a name like that, he'll probably grow into a wrecking ball."

I shook my head and laughed with him. "Not 'gentle.' Jentil with a J… Like the pagan giants in Basque mythology." I stroked the puppy's back. "They were big and strong and lived in the mountains."

He smiled and sipped his coffee. "Basque mythology." He set his cup down on the table and shook his head. "I'm guessing you went to school *somewhere*." He took the puppy from my hands, and this time when it cried, Josh shushed him. "Settle down, Jentil." He set him back down on the blanket in his box. "Eat some breakfast," he told me. "You're gonna need your energy to get through a morning with Avery."

The mention of her name brought the image of her face to my mind, and inexplicable dread crept like a shadow across my thoughts. Careful not to speak ill of one of his friends, especially one who'd been so kind to me, I forced a smile until I could hide my mouth behind my coffee cup. It was going to be a long morning.

~

When Josh pulled into the parking lot, puffs of exhaust were already rising up from the tailpipe of Avery's idling Subaru. He backed the truck up alongside her car and rolled the window down. She rolled hers down too. "Don't say it," she warned him, her voice vibrating as she shivered.

"It's not even October!" he said.

"I don't want to hear it! I'm freezing!" She looked past him to me. "You ready, Paige?" I pushed out a grin and nodded. Avery beckoned me with the tilt of her head. "Well, come on! I need some coffee and a cookie!"

"Okay!" I lifted the puppy to my lips and gave him a goodbye kiss. "Bye-bye, Jentil. I'll be back," I promised. When I turned to open the door, Josh put his hand on my arm.

"Do *I* get a goodbye?" His eyes were so sincere they melted my heart.

"Of course." I leaned across the seat and met him halfway. As our lips touched, his big hand caressed my cheek. We pulled apart, and he whispered, "I lo—" He paused for a moment, then smiled wide and sat back in his seat. "I look forward to seeing you this afternoon. Get something nice. Whatever you need."

I nodded. "Thank you. I lo… look forward to seeing you too." We shared a smile as I slipped out of the truck.

Avery must have sensed my discomfort when I climbed into her car. "Don't worry, Paige. We're gonna have a lot of fun." She patted my knee. "I need a distraction too."

I nodded as she backed the car out of the parking lot, but I didn't believe her.

Whisper Cove was tiny. As we drove down Water Street, it became clear that one of the reasons Avery's bar probably did so well, besides her sparkling personality, was its advantageous distinction of being the one and only watering hole in the entire town. Even if one didn't like sparkling personalities, there was nowhere else to go.

There were more empty shops than open businesses. A single stone building served as the town hall, post office, notary public, and barber shop. A sign posted in the window with a barber pole painted on it read, "Tuesday 7am - Noon" and "Thursday Noon - 4pm."

A Catholic church, which looked more like a summer home with a steeple thrown on, sat back from the road. Further along, a decaying gazebo sat in the center of the town square next to an odd sculpture of two giant hands shaking. Faded letters on a sign mounted by a stone entrance read, "Breakwater Park." Beyond that, a massive community theater stood crumbling on its last legs with a sign that read, "December 10th - The Nutcracker."

"Wow," I said before I could stop myself. "There's nothing here."

Avery nodded. "Nothing but people. And not very many of them."

"Why are there so many empty stores? It looks like it used to be a busy place."

"It did," she said, turning onto Shipwreck Road, "but that was way before my time. Back in the eighteen hundreds, this was a quarry town."

"A quarry town?" I raised my eyebrows, and she nodded. "What did they quarry?"

"Granite. If you drive all the way down Driftwood Lane, just past the old Tuttle house, there's a dirt road that leads to a granite quarry right by the water. They used to mine the granite and ship it out all over the world. Men came from every corner of the earth to work here. Then women came too. Maine's own version of a boom town."

"What happened to everyone?"

Avery shrugged. "What happens to everything—time marches on."

We came to an intersection on the outskirts of town, and she turned left down a road marked "Beach Rose Crossing." The first driveway we came to sat outside a big white farmhouse, and Avery pulled in there.

It was a lot like Josh's house, only bigger, and it appeared to have been built over time with sections added through the years. A hand-painted sign was posted by the front door. "Goat Milk Soap and Beeswax Candles."

Avery slapped my bare leg. "Come on. Let's get you come clothes before you freeze to death."

I shook my head and looked the sprawling farmhouse over. "Here?"

"Don't judge a book by its cover, Paige. Leave that job to the boys." She winked and grabbed her purse from between the seats. "Let's go. Chloe's got coffee and macadamia nut cookies waiting for us."

I followed Avery out of the car and up the steps to the

front door, which opened before we even had a chance to knock. Standing with a wide, welcoming grin on her face, a pretty little blond woman in her early twenties stood with her hands supporting the small of her back and an enormous baby bump sticking out in front. "You should just send your paycheck straight to me, Avery," she said with a wry grin.

Avery laughed and stepped inside. "I know, I know. I have an addiction." I followed her through the door, and she turned and put her arm around me. "Chloe, this is Paige. Paige, meet Chloe. Chloe, Paige needs a little bit of everything. Paige, Chloe's got a little bit of everything you need."

We smiled and exchanged nods.

Chloe shut the door behind us and walked down the front hall of the big house with Avery and me trailing behind. "It's a good thing you called when you did." As she waddled ahead of us, it was impossible to miss how uncomfortable her every step was. "I have a feeling this little guy's not gonna stay put much longer."

"What does the doctor say?" Avery asked

Chloe laughed and tucked her short blond hair behind one ear. "The doctor? There's two hours of potholes and no bathrooms between me and the nearest doctor." She opened a door at the end of the hall and stepped aside. "Josh tells me I've got another two weeks, but I find that hard to believe."

"My Josh?" I asked, forgetting it was a secret. *Is it a secret?*

Chloe laughed and her eyes opened wide. "*Your* Josh?" She turned to Avery. "I've only been on maternity leave a week."

Avery shrugged and walked past her into the room. "Like I was telling Paige in the car, time marches on."

I followed Avery to find myself stepping into another world. Unlike the old, rustic New England feel that permeated the rest of the house, this room was modern and ultra-feminine with straight lines in varying shades of cream and soft pink and silver accent pieces throughout. An overstuffed lavender sofa sat in the center of the room on a white faux fur rug surrounded on three sides by racks of clothes.

"Some of it is one-of-a-kind. Some of it, I find in the far corners of the internet." Chloe stroked her swollen baby bump and smiled. "If you find something you like, don't be put off if the size isn't right. I may have what you need out back… like at a shoe store. There's only so much room in this old place."

Avery tapped me on the shoulder. "If she doesn't have it out back, she can make it for you."

Chloe held up her hand. "I don't work with deadlines, though. Not with a baby coming." She waddled around the room, pointing at various displays as we followed her. "As you see, your basic jeans, slacks, blouses, skirts, and all that are on the racks. Over here," she rested her hand on a glass case, "I keep the panties and bras. The case is just to keep the dust off them. You can open it right up if you see something you like."

"That's my favorite part." Avery bounced up and down like a schoolgirl on a shopping spree.

"Men's gifts like cologne and gloves are in the back room. Over here," she motioned toward a tall wood table against the white and silver wall, "I have women's perfumes. Try not to spray if you can resist. You can smell them inside the caps." She offered an apologetic grin. "Strong smells make my little guy sick."

Avery ran ahead of me to the perfume display and grabbed a small, ornately etched bottle with a gold tassel dangling at the side. "Here!" Her blue eyes shined as brightly as her enormous smile. Something about the way the light from the crystal chandelier shimmered on the glossy surface of her red lips caught my eye. She turned to me, popped the cap off the bottle, and held it under my nose. "You smell that?"

I stared at her, and for a moment, she wasn't Avery, and we weren't in Chloe's backroom boutique. We were two thousand miles away, just inside the entrance of the Wrong Way Tavern. Amid the loud voices, the endless commotion, and the heavy rock music blaring from the overhead speakers, a girl with long black hair and glossy red lips turned to me, smiling. "You smell that?" she asked.

Caught between the *then* and *now*, I could barely draw a breath. "Melody," I whispered.

Josh

Caleb sat perfectly still, his tablet and computer set up on the bar in front of him. Tiny bubbles rose from the lime he'd shoved down the neck of his Corona. Patiently, he watched me from behind hooded eyes as I turned the icy mug of Shipyard in my hands and made the foam slosh out over the rim.

"This memory…" I started and then stopped to think my words through. "Do you think it was a boyfriend? A husband? Who is she running from?" I turned and eyed him beseechingly, begging for answers I knew he didn't have.

Caleb leaned back, his eyes now hidden under the brim of his ever-present ball cap. "Josh, buddy, there is no real way to know until we figure out who she is. There are a lot of blonde women her age in the US." I opened my mouth, and he just held up a hand. "I'm searching missing persons right now, but the truck is stolen, so I'm looking at not only North Dakota but the states around it. That's a lot of law enforcement databases to go through."

I let out a gusty sigh. The not knowing was eating away at me like a cancer in the pit of my stomach. "I know, and I appreciate your help. I just… Did some guy hurt her? Is that why she's here?" I dropped my head into my hands, overwhelmed by the uncertainty and the possibility she was still in danger. "Did they run her off the road? Do they know where she is? Will they be after her?"

Caleb shifted on the tippy bar stool, reaching one foot out on the brass foot bar to steady himself, and put a hand on my shoulder. "You can't think like that, Josh. She's here, and she's safe. If it's a guy, Logan will know what to do. Here…" Caleb picked up the tablet, making the screen light up, and swiped to open a file. "Look through these. See if any of them are Paige. Doing nothing always makes it worse."

I looked down at the tiled pictures on the screen. "All these women are missing?" With one finger, I scrolled through dozens of images: blondes, brunettes, redheads, old, young, fat, thin. Each one was reported missing by a friend or loved one.

Caleb glanced toward the door, the bell tinkling and announcing the arrival of Mack and Ma for their daily lunch break. We both waved and smiled at the older couple, then buried our heads back in our own business.

"Josh, at any given time, about 90,000 people are missing in the US. Roughly half of them are female. If your Paige is one of them, we will find her, but it takes time."

"She's not *my* Paige." Irritated, I flipped through more images. "I just—what horrible thing brought her to Whisper Cove? And is it coming after her?"

"Josh!" Caleb rocked his bar stool back on two legs. "If Paige was in an abusive relationship, it was a huge step for her to leave. She did the right thing." The chair dropped forward with a thud. "If it's something else, we'll figure that out too, but I need you to focus. All this 'what if?' stuff isn't going to help. We need action. Step one—we search missing persons. Step two—we search BOLOs and wanted files. If we need to, we'll figure out a 'step three.' But you have two jobs right now: to drink that Shipyard, and to look at those photos. Paige is safe. Trust me—no one wants to cross Avery. Now drink." He raised a hand, hailing the young woman waiting tables, and ordered us each another drink and a plate of nachos.

I looked around the room at all the patrons. Most were local. Mack and Ma shared a sandwich by the window. Owen sat with some slick looking thirty-somethings, probably campaign advisors, looking over papers on the table between them. Daniel relaxed in the corner, a plate of picked-clean Buffalo wings in front of him. This was my town, and these were my people.

Caleb was right. I needed to get my head out of my ass. I just wasn't used to my life turning upside down like this. I wasn't accustomed to worrying about another person. A new appreciation for the familiar grew inside me. I liked a life of no surprises.

But then my eyes narrowed as the bar door opened, and two strangers walked in. With long dark hair and simple clothes, they could have been anything from civil servants to construction workers. I only knew they weren't from Whisper Cove, and that made me nervous.

I watched them as they sat at a tall table and ordered, laughing with the waitress as she flirted for tips. The muscles in my arms tensed, and I clenched my jaw. I didn't like the look of them, and strangers in my town made me mad. It was a new and strange reaction, but I couldn't shake it. *What if they're looking for Paige?*

Chapter Twelve

Paige

I didn't remember her. Not really. I could see her face in my mind and hear those three little words, "You smell that?" Useless. It was just a fragment of a memory. However, it opened the floodgate to an ocean of fragments that began to pour into my consciousness. Bars, kitchens, faces, laughter, tears, worries, funerals, and celebrations—I saw them all one second at a time. None of them made any sense, but they all filled me with emotions.

I stood there in the boutique, crippled by my thoughts as Avery did her best to gather the essentials for me. "What's your bra size?" she asked, but I didn't know. "Jeans or dresses?" I couldn't remember.

My thoughts a millions miles away, I stared absently at the pile of clothes she and Chloe had gathered and said, "I want to see Josh."

By the time Chloe had boxed and bagged everything and Avery had driven us back to the bar, the random snapshots of my former life had taken over my mind, filling all the empty spaces and forcing out the peace Josh had helped me find. I threw the door open the moment the car stopped, and raced inside to find him sitting with Caleb at a makeshift office on the bar. He turned his head to me, and when I looked into his pale blue eyes, I fell apart.

Caleb didn't even look up from his laptop before he started talking. "Paige, there's a missing person's report out of Neb—"

"What's wrong?" Josh's face whitened at the sight of me. He slipped from his stool and wrapped his arms around me. "What happened? Are you okay?"

"No." My cry was barely a squeak. "I'm not okay."

Before Caleb could fill me in on the details of his discovery, Josh led me out to the truck, and I sat in the cab while he fetched the bags and boxes from Avery's tailgate. On the ride home, he listened quietly as I wept and tried to explain. "They're my life! Little pieces of my life! But they don't make sense! And they don't feel good!" I turned my tired eyes to him. "I felt so good this morning. I want to be her again."

He lifted my hand and held it against his cheek as we turned onto Seaglass Drive. "Who, baby?"

"Me! The me with a puppy! The me in the big farmhouse in the middle of nowhere! The me you love!"

Josh kissed my hand. "You *are* the you I love." He pulled the car into the driveway, drove down between the fieldstone fences to the house, and parked. "I don't care who you were," he said. "I care who you *are*. If your head is full of nonsense, I'll help you make sense of it all."

"What if who I am is awful?"

He shook his head. "Paige Elizabeth Carlisle, I already know who you are. There's nothing awful in you." Josh wrapped a hand behind my head and pulled me in close to place a kiss on my forehead. "Come in. Let me help you."

"Paige Elizabeth Carlisle?" The moment I said it aloud, I knew it was right.

He nodded. "We found you. Come inside, and I'll tell you who you are."

Trembling with terror, confused and despondent, I let Josh lead me by the hand into the house.

It's surreal to hear your life story as told by someone else while having no first-hand recollection of the tale. Side by side on the couch, he held my hand, and I stared at the shape and movement of his lips as he told of my parents, my siblings, my hometown, even my career. He might as well have been telling me about another woman, a stranger to us both. By the time he'd finished reporting what Caleb's investigation had turned up, I felt he knew me better than I knew myself.

There was something Josh wasn't telling me, though. I could sense it in the spaces between his words. Over the next month, as Caleb learned more, Josh took on the role of filter, sorting the good discoveries from the bad and only sharing what he thought I could handle. Maybe I should have demanded more, but I was already clinging to the edge of sanity, and I was afraid that any more bad news would be so heavy, my fingers would slip, and I'd freefall into madness.

Josh must have sensed my fragility because he never pushed me. Instead, he entrusted me with Jentil's care, and soon my little puppy was bigger and stronger, and our fears he would wither away were forgotten. Keeping him in puppy formula became a full-time job.

With Chloe gone from the clinic's reception desk, our time alone was limited, so I rode to work with him every day and helped manage appointments and patients in her absence. It gave us more time together and lifted from his shoulders the burden of paperwork, for which he had no talent. I guess my time as a social worker had prepared me for the endless shuffling of forms and charts because I managed in minutes what would have taken him hours.

After work, we'd take Jentil down to Avery's bar and pretend he was a service dog in training while relaxing over beers with Caleb, Logan, and Owen. Josh's friends became my friends, and I was so grateful to know them all. Even Mack and Ma, who I knew would eventually want their puppy back, became familiars I looked forward to seeing.

Alone at home, we'd take long walks along Seaglass Drive, which led east to a rocky shore where we'd sit and talk for hours or just sit quietly and watch the sun go down. Then we'd walk back to the house, and I'd make dinner while Josh started a fire. Eventually, we'd end up in bed, lying naked in each other's arms, blissful. Perfect.

It was at the beginning of just such a day that I pulled my sweaty body from Josh's side and strolled down the hall with a couple fresh towels in my arms. I may have been humming. I don't recall. I just know the bathroom was warm, and when I wiped the steam from the mirror, I liked the woman staring back at me.

I stepped under the showerhead and let the hot water fall over me. With long, lazy strokes, I lathered myself from head to toe, rinsed, and pasted conditioner in my wavy blond locks. Then it started.

Before I even realized there was a song in my head, I opened my mouth and began to sing.

Josh

I couldn't remember ever being that happy. The soothing sound of the water droplets hitting the tile in the bathroom shower complimented my thoughts as I lay there. The cotton sheets felt crisp against my skin and smelled of sunshine and Paige. A ray of light in my life, she seamlessly fit in and cast a glow on everything she touched.

That past month had been like a dream, and I was so grateful to have lived it. Being the highest ranking medical professional in town was draining. I loved each and every one of our 713 (soon to be 714) residents, but someone always needed something. Paige, on the other hand, cared for *me*, and it had been so long since anyone had catered to *my* needs. Too long. And I loved her for it.

My eyes drifted around the room, appreciating all the tiny bits of herself she left scattered around my world. The black lace bra decorated with tiny pink ribbons hung off one arm of the rocking chair. A butterfly barrette she often pulled her long, blond hair back in sat next to her hair brush and lipstick on the simple white vanity I'd brought home for her. Jentil, who was so much more hers than mine or Mack's or Ma's, slept in the box she'd decorated with blue bows and a handmade sign with his name painted in cursive. Everything Paige touched, she made more beautiful. Even the vase of late season flowers she'd found on one of our hikes and set on the window sill brought a splash of color to the house. She made everything just a little brighter, a little lovelier. Her unique palette painted my world and brought joy to my heart each and every time I looked at her. My life was no longer a black and white existence, not with Paige in it.

My ears perked at the thud of the pipes as Paige turned off the water in the shower. I heard the slap of her wet feet on the scarred wood floors as she charged down the hall and into the bedroom. Water drops fell everywhere around her and pooled at her feet, and a crazy big grin graced her face.

I pulled the sheet up to hide my reaction at the sight of her. I didn't need her to think that's all this was—sex—but I was too slow.

She quirked up a corner of her mouth, raising one eyebrow and licking her already shiny lips. A small groan escaped me as the tent between my legs rose another story. We both froze, and I prayed she would make the first move.

The fluffy white bath towel Paige had wrapped herself in slipped from her fingers and fell to the floor in slow motion, landing in a heap at her feet. Delicately, she lifted one foot and stepped over it. Her hips swayed as she approached the bed, and her seductive movements hypnotized me. I couldn't tear my eyes away.

"Is that for me?" Like a jungle cat she dropped to her knees and crawled across the bed, her eyes turning a dark emerald green with desire. "What is under here?" She playfully tugged at the sheet, pulling it down inch by inch until my manhood sprung free, pointing to the sky.

She made a purring noise deep in her throat and ducked her head, licking my length like an ice cream cone.

"Ohhhhhh," I arched my back as pleasure shot through me.

"Don't move. It's my turn." She took me in her hand, slopped her lazy tongue over the head of my cock, and stroked me from base to tip.

"You're incredible," I told her, watching her work. This was a new Paige, a confident Paige.

"Guess what I discovered," she said, holding me like a microphone, her breath tickling the very tip of my throbbing member and making me squirm.

"What?" I asked, breathless and transfixed by the naughty things her hand and mouth were doing to me.

"I can sing!" Without even waiting for me to respond to her announcement she engulfed me in her mouth, stroking faster, bobbing up and down. All thoughts left my mind as she decadently laved me with her tongue.

"Paige," I started to sit up, trying to focus, but she stopped me, placing her free hand in the center of my chest, her mouth on me, never stopping.

"No," she warbled around me, my length deep in her throat. The vibrations rolled down my shaft to my groin and made my balls draw up even tighter. I collapsed back on the bed, my arms outstretched. I stared up at the ceiling and wondered how I'd gotten so lucky.

I felt her shift, sliding up my legs, my shaft bereft of both her mouth and hands and then suddenly—heaven. My tip met her center, and she lowered herself inch by inch, taking me into her until I was seated to the hilt.

"Oh my God," I groaned as she began to move. Held down by invisible shackles, I lay there and let her ride me. This Paige was glorious, a strong woman taking what she wanted. She rose and fell, grinding her clit against me every time she sheathed me.

"Almost…" she ground out, riding me faster. Her gorgeous breasts swayed with every gyration of her curvy hips. I about swallowed my tongue as I felt the sweet pressure between us build. It grew and spread, winding around my cock, heating my groin, until it was almost unbearable.

"I'm close…" I cried, my back arching, my pelvis thrusting to meet her stroke for stroke.

She threw her head back and let out a yell. "Josh!" Her walls spasmed around me and pushed me over the edge of my release. I cried out my orgasm, and we came together, wave after wave. Each movement slowed and grew more languid. The distinction between us blurring until it seemed we were truly one.

A few moments later, Paige stilled. A knowing smile blossomed on her face as she leaned forward and looked down into my eyes. She lowered herself to place a slow kiss on my lips before sitting up, swinging herself off me, and severing our connection.

Casually, she sashayed over to pick up her towel. "I'll meet you downstairs in a minute." With her glorious ass facing me, she looked over her shoulder and held my gaze as she turned back to the door with a wink.

"Thank you for the flowers." I whispered to her retreating back.

Chapter Thirteen

Paige

Smile, Paige.

I wasn't unhappy. In fact, I was floating through life on a cloud of pure bliss. The only problem with being that joyful, that peaceful, that in love was the sense that just beyond the perfection, something terrible was still waiting for me. My life was a beautiful dream that I knew I was doomed to wake from.

As I danced around the kitchen that morning, starting the coffee and whipping up pancake batter from a fragmented memory of a family recipe, the song from the shower echoed in my head. I hummed its melody as I cracked the eggs and sang the words while bacon crackled on one side of the cast iron hot plate. *This road rolls on forever…*

Josh wandered into the kitchen just as I was pouring two mugs of coffee at the table. He waited until I set the carafe down on the trivet and then herded me back against the counter and penned me in between his arms. He kissed my left cheek, then my right, and topped it off with a tiny peck on the tip of my nose. "Watcha singing, blondie?" he whispered in my ear.

His breath tickled, and I giggled. "I don't know. Just something stuck in my head."

Burying his face in my hair, he drew a deep breath through his nose. "I love it." He wrapped his arms around me and devoured my neck, which made me squeal with delight. That made Jentil pop his head up from the patchwork pillow bed he'd dragged over by the stove and announced his presence with the tiniest, sweetest bark. Josh looked down at him and playfully growled back. "I'll share the bacon, but *she's* mine."

Yap! Yap!

"Okay," he said with a sigh of resignation, "I'll share her too." With one last kiss, Josh began prepping Jentil's formula, and I turned back to flip the pancakes.

That song stayed in my head and on my lips all through breakfast. *Me and no one but my crew… riding down the avenue…* It was so dominant in my thoughts there came a point when I stopped fighting it and just let it out despite the fact that poor Josh had heard the same six lines thirty times in a row. He didn't complain, though. Eventually, he began to sing along.

We sang them as I cleaned up after breakfast, and he swept the living room floor. We sang them as we covered his grandmother's cedar bushes in burlap to protect them from the coming winter. We were still singing them as we assembled the leftover breakfast bacon into lunch BLTs. When I remembered more words, we sang those too.

Our life was a joy, but that sense of impending disaster never went away… not for me, anyhow. That day, its weight was especially heavy. After we'd eaten, I told Josh I was tired. "Must have been all the chores," I said innocently.

"Go take a nap." He picked up the last crumbles of bacon on his plate and popped them in his mouth. "It's Saturday. We have nowhere to be until tonight."

I nodded. "I think I'll probably need a little extra energy if I'm going to keep up with Avery. I love her, but she wears me out."

He laughed. "Small doses sometimes."

I left him at the table, and as I climbed the stairs to the bedroom, I could hear the clang of our dirty dishes in the sink and that song still on his lips. *The roar of the engine... The purr of my woman...* He sounded so content it brought a smile to my face.

Pulling the shades down made the room just dark enough for a quick afternoon nap. As I crawled under the blankets, I realized I wasn't just tired—I was completely exhausted. I lay there, staring at the ceiling, and it dawned on me that what I was feeling wasn't a nagging sense of dread but fear. For the first time in weeks, I was genuinely afraid, but I didn't know what scared me.

The pictures in your head? No. None of the stills were particularly frightening. There was the vision of the girl—the one who looked like Avery—asking me about a smell, but that wasn't scary. The flashback of the angry man's face had been terrifying when it had first appeared to me, but that was so long ago its power over me had faded. Other than that, my old life was just snapshots too far out of context to mean anything to me.

Comforted knowing Josh was right downstairs if I needed him, I closed my eyes and eventually drifted off to sleep. My dreams were lovely absurdities about puppies, babies, burlap, and snow. When I woke an hour later, the room was still shadowed, the day was still young, and I was entirely refreshed.

I descended the stairs with a yawn to find the living room vacant and the whole house silent. Making my way to kitchen to start a fresh pot of coffee, I found Josh sitting at the table with his laptop open and his headphones on. Before he could see me, I crept up behind him and landed a surprise kiss on the top of his head. With his height, I hardly ever got a chance to do that.

At the touch of my lips, he reached behind his chair and wrapped his hands around the back of my thighs to hold me in place. "How was your nap?"

"I feel like a new woman," I said. "You want some coffee?"

"Always." He released my legs, and I made my way to the coffee maker, grabbed the glass pot, and carried it to the sink. I turned the water on and held the pot under the faucet.

"I found something while you were asleep," he said.

I looked back over my shoulder to see his handsome smile and his blue eyes sparkling. Sometimes he looked like such an enormous little boy I couldn't help but laugh. "What did you find?"

He pulled the headphones from his ears and set them on the table. Then he pulled the cord from the jack on his laptop. "This." He pushed a button on the keyboard, and a steady beat filled the kitchen.

Shutting the faucet off, I turned from the sink and stood listening with the full pot in my hand. The beat gained speed and volume until it seemed to match the beat of my heart… or my heart changed its beat to match the rhythm. It seemed familiar, but I couldn't place it until the guitars entered.

It was the song I'd been singing—*we'd* been singing—all morning. Only, it was different. I'd remembered it wrong. It wasn't a love song or a slow ballad. It was hard and fast heavy metal. I remembered the melody, but the feeling that came with it was sheer terror. "Stop it, Josh," I said as I felt myself turn pale. But Josh didn't hear me.

Then the vocals kicked in. They weren't soft or bluesy as I'd recalled them, but hateful and threatening. *The road rolls on forever… we'll stop at nothing, never… too many scores to settle… with leather, guns, and metal...*

All at once, it came back to me. Or *I* came back to *it.* We were in that dark bar, Melody and I, staring straight into that pockmarked face with the crooked nose and beady black eyes. His lips were moving, only this time, I could hear his voice—low and scarred. "Blood for blood, bitch," he said, looking so deep into my eyes my skin crawled. "You're gonna beg me to kill you by the time I'm done."

Back in the kitchen, in the *now*, far from the smoky bar with neon beer signs, my body weakened, my lips trembled, and the glass coffee pot slipped through my sweaty grasp. It landed on the hardwood floor with *crash* that sent shards of glass and water flying in all directions.

Josh

"Paige? Paige, are you okay?" My jaw dropped when she turned bone white, dropping the coffee pot, spreading broken glass over every inch of the kitchen.

Her eyes glossed over as if her mind went somewhere else, and her mouth opened and closed in a silent scream.

I ran to her as she bent over and emptied the contents of her stomach on my feet, the hot liquid rushing out with a roar, splattering across the wood floor, mixing with the shattered glass and splashing my pant legs.

"Paige!" I crouched down beside her and held her hair back as she retched over and over before finally collapsing in my arms. Tears ran from her eyes, and saliva, snot, and puke dripped from her mouth and nose. I reached behind me and grabbed the hand towel from the back of a kitchen chair, and used it to gently wipe her mouth. She took it from me, wiping her eyes and loudly blowing her nose before sinking into the closest chair.

"I'm sorry."

"Don't be sorry. What's going on?"

"He's going to kill me," she whispered.

"Who? Who's going to kill you?"

"The man." She sobbed and began to pant. "The man is going to kill me!" Her arms grabbed for me, and she continued to babble nonsensically, her eyes wild, and her breathing fast and shallow.

I pulled my phone from my pocket, and speed dialed Logan.

"Josh Dalton," he said when he picked up.

"Hey, get here as soon as you can," I shouted the minute he answered. "Paige is freaking out. She keeps repeating that some man is going to kill her. I need everybody here."

After Logan promised he was on his way with lights and sirens, I hung up and turned my attention back to Paige. "Come on, let's get you cleaned up." I scooped her up off the chair, carrying her up the stairs and into bathroom, stepping gingerly around the puddle of vomit, my boots crunching across the glass I couldn't avoid.

"Here," I sat her on the toilet and began to undress her like a child. I slipped her shoes from her feet, setting them just outside the door. Turning the water on, I filled the tub as I peeled her messy jeans down her legs. "Arms up." She raised them robotically, wordlessly following my orders. *What the hell was she involved in?*

I had just tucked her into the water when I heard someone knocking at the kitchen door. "Josh! It's me!" Hollering as he let himself in, I heard Logan walk through the kitchen and stop at the bottom of the steps.

"Upstairs! I'll be right down!" I looked Paige over and ran a soft washcloth over her face to clean the mess away. "Can you get dressed by yourself?" She nodded dumbly. "Come down when you're ready, okay? I'm going to go talk to Logan."

Thumping down the steps, one hand trailing along the

polished wood bannister, I turned the corner and found both Caleb and Logan sitting in the living room.

"Hey, guys, thanks for coming so quick." I huffed out a deep breath and flopped onto the couch next to Logan.

"You sounded pretty frantic on the phone." Logan pointed back over his shoulder. "The kitchen's in a state. What happened?"

"We were in the kitchen, and Paige has been singing this song, and I found it on the computer. I played it for her, and she flipped out. She started rambling about a man killing her. She couldn't breathe and started throwing up. I didn't know what to do."

"Can I talk to her?" Logan asked, pulling out his notebook and flipping it open.

"Yeah, she'll be down in a minute."

"Guys, I think I know what she remembered." I had almost forgotten Caleb was there, he had been so quiet the whole time.

Logan and I both looked over at him, knowing there was no point in pushing—he'd share when he was ready.

He pulled his laptop from his messenger bag and set it up on the coffee table. "Look here."

A newspaper article appeared on the screen with a picture of the meanest, nastiest looking dude I'd ever seen. "Notorious Bike Gang Leader Murdered in Local Bar," I mumbled as I read the headline.

"It's about a biker gang in North Dakota—the Hell Dogs. Two days before Paige crashed into Whisper Cove, the gang's leader was killed in a scuffle at a bar in Williston."

Searing pain shot through my head. Paige didn't look anything like a biker's old lady. "Jesus. Who have I let into my life?"

"Into the town," Logan added. "It's starting to sound like she's mixed up in more than you can handle."

"Look at this guy." Caleb scrolled down. "The man

suspected of the killing looks just like the man Paige described, right down to the greasy hair dangling around his face."

Logan reached into his briefcase, pulled out the sketch, and held it up. The images were nearly identical. "That's incredible."

Who have I fallen in love with?

Chapter Fourteen

Paige

I soaked until the bathwater ran cool and considered draining it and starting all over again. Downstairs, the three of them waited for me, for details I didn't want to give them. They weren't pretty or easy. My life, as I was remembering it, didn't fit with Whisper Cove's small town, wholesome vibe.

The song I'd so carelessly sung all morning and shared like a fool with the man I loved was the glue that that joined a thousand little puzzle pieces I'd been carrying in my mind for the last month. Altogether, the picture was a horror show that I didn't want to share with anyone. Paige Elizabeth Carlisle's life was a nightmare, and no sane person—lover or friend—would want anything to do with her monsters.

As I stared at my red toenails sticking up from the surface of the cold water, I wanted desperately to go back in time to that morning. *Forget those words and never sing them again!* But it was too late. I knew everything, and I owed Josh every ugly detail.

I pulled the plug and watched the water drain from the

tub as silent tears ran down my cheeks. My memories were so terrifying I'd driven halfway across the country to escape them, but they weren't nearly as frightening as telling Josh the truth. This time, though, I wouldn't run.

I descended the staircase in fresh clothes with my head held high. They were all sitting in the living room, staring at Caleb's computer, so engrossed they didn't notice my arrival. My chin up, I cleared my throat, and they all turned their attention to me.

Josh came to his feet. "Here. Sit down, babe." He took my arm, but I gently shrugged him off.

"*You* need to sit down, Josh," I said firmly, somberly. He took one look in my eyes and eased himself back down into the overstuffed chair. With all eyes focused on me, I took a deep breath and began a story I hadn't edited or rehearsed. I just had to tell them everything.

"You all know my name, my job, and where I'm from, but you don't know what happened."

In the quiet of their attention, I looked down and took a deep breath before I went on. My lips moved to form words before my thoughts and voice caught up. Then, finally, it all came together.

"Williston is a fracking town. There's a lot of money and a lot of lonely men." I glanced at Josh as my stomach turned. "There are also a lot of desperate women. That's a tragic combination."

"Were you one of them?" Caleb asked, reminding me Josh and I weren't alone.

I shook my head. "No, but my sister was—Melody. She was the reason I was there. I'm not from North Dakota. I grew up in a quiet little corn field in Nebraska. Melody is—" I choked on the word, "—*was* my father's daughter. He had worked just outside the Fort Berthold reservation. That's where Melody grew up."

Josh leaned forward at the edge of his seat. "You were visiting her?"

Tears that had welled in my eyes spilled over as I shook my head. I wiped them away with a sniff. "No. I went to Williston to save her."

"Save her from what?" Logan asked without a hint of emotion on his stern face.

"The Hell Dogs. When my father was dying—" I laughed absurdly through the tears. "Jesus. I forgot my father was dead." From the corner of my eye, I saw Josh hang his head, and I knew that was one of the discoveries he'd been keeping secret from me. "When he was dying, he told me about Melody. After he passed, I didn't know what else to do with myself, so I spent a month searching for her, and when I found her, I knew I had to help her."

"W-what was wrong with her?" Josh asked, his hand half-covering his mouth to hide his shocked expression.

"Everything. She was a prostitute. She was property of the bikers. She told me she wanted to get out, but she didn't know how." I laughed at myself. "And I was naïve. I'd never been anywhere bigger than Omaha, and I didn't know what... monsters... were out there. Or that my own sister could be one."

Caleb sighed and rubbed the back of his neck. "We all let our families down sometimes."

"No," I shook my head. "She didn't let me down. She set me up."

"What do you mean?" Logan's hard glare never softened.

"I drove up there to Williston and met Melody at a coffee shop." I thought back to that afternoon, her striking face and dark black hair, and the vision took my breath away. "She was gorgeous. Half Sioux with the most stunning features. Green eyes like my father's... like mine. Only they were so... captivating against her dark skin."

"Paige." Logan's hard voice brought me back to the moment. "What happened?"

Unable to look at Josh, I stared back at Logan, taking strength from his cold expression. "She told me she had to go to work. I begged her not to go. I told her my car was outside and that she could leave with me right then. I'd take her back to Nebraska, and she'd never have to see the men who made her do that ever again. But she said it didn't work that way. She said they would find her. They'd hunt her down and bring her back. They'd hurt her and everyone she loved. She said no one ever got away from them—not ever."

"And then?"

"She said to meet her back at one of the bars that night. I thought we'd meet for a drink, and I could talk some sense into her, but when I got to the bar, the whole parking lot was full of motorcycles. I parked my car and stared at the building for a long time." Groaning at the memory, I cradled my head in my hands. "I knew I shouldn't go in. I knew I was in way over my head, but…"

"But?" Josh whispered.

"But she was my sister. My father was dead, and she was the only family I had in the whole world."

"So you went in," Caleb said.

I nodded. "The whole place was a mess. Wall to wall leather jackets. Broken glass and trash on the floor. Drugs on the tables. There was a stage in the front with naked women dancing. One of them was my Melody. When she saw me, she looked to someone off to her side, a man with long, greasy blond hair, and she pointed at me. He nodded, and she stepped down from the stage and came to see me. She gave me a big hug."

I curled my lip thinking back to that night. "There was this odor all through the place. When she hugged me, I could smell it in her hair. I pulled back from her, and I must have made a funny face because she smiled and said, 'You smell that? That's the smell of money.'"

"What did it smell like?" Logan asked.

"I don't know. I'd never smelled it before. Acid, maybe. Ammonia."

"Meth," Caleb said. "They were probably cooking it."

"What happened next?" I turned to see Josh with his hands folded over his mouth and his eyes narrowed in anger. I'd never seen him like that, and the look made me weep again.

"She took me out back… to a room away from the music. She said she wanted to talk to me about getting out… but the blond man followed us. And when we got to the room, there was another man already waiting for us…" I trailed off as I sank into the memory of that horrible night. "He was surrounded by money and little baggies. He had cruel eyes—so small I could barely see them."

"And then what?"

"Melody stepped back against the wall, and the two men came at me. They grabbed me, but I fought. The big guy—the one who was waiting for us out back when we got there—I remember his fist coming at my face. Then everything was dark for a second. The next thing I remember, I opened my eyes, and they were talking to Melody, not even paying attention to me. I needed to get out, but they were blocking the door. I saw a knife forgotten on a table in the middle of everything, and I grabbed it."

"You took his knife?" Logan asked.

"I held it up, pointed it at them. I told them to get out of my way, to let me go or I'd stab them, but they didn't believe me. The big guy came at me again… with his hands out like he was going to grab me… so I swung the knife. The first time, I missed, and they all laughed at me. Even Melody laughed. The men kept threatening, taunting me with the things they would do to me."

Logan nodded. "The second time?"

I stared him dead in the eye. "I swung it higher. I could tell he didn't think I was a threat. This time it caught him in the throat." I turned to Josh, desperate to see his reaction, praying he wouldn't be as disgusted with me as I was with myself, but his hands hid his mouth, and all I could see was his wide blue eyes. "He fell to the ground with his hands on his neck. And blood sprayed everywhere."

"Then what?" Logan asked.

"The blonde man told me I'd be sorry for that. He pulled a knife from a sheath on his belt and plunged it into Melody's heart." My voice cracked. "She fell to the floor… her big green eyes just staring at me as the blood pooled around her body. I couldn't do anything. I couldn't save her."

Josh shook his head in disbelief. "How the hell did you get out of there?"

"I pointed the bloody knife at the blond guy. He stared at me. 'Blood for blood,' he snarled."

"And?"

"He said before he was done, I'd beg him to kill me. I didn't give him a chance to pull his knife from Melody's chest. I stabbed him in the arm… and I ran straight out the back. There was a group of them—the bikers—out by a big cattle hauler, herding a bunch of women inside. I ran in the opposite direction. There was a truck on the side of the building, idling. I didn't know whose it was. I just knew it had keys in it, so I jumped in. As I drove away, I saw the back door to the club open, and the blond man run out."

Josh

She watched her sister die.

I couldn't stop thinking about Paige's story. I couldn't

imagine what she'd gone through. No wonder she didn't want to remember and blocked it all out. *My God, she's a survivor.*

"Hey, look at this." Caleb turned the screen to show me a grainy black-and-white image. He'd found an FBI bulletin for an unknown female wanted for questioning in the death of the president of the Hell Dogs biker gang.

I just stared. There was no doubt in my mind that the woman in the photo was Paige. The curve of her cheek, the flow of her hair, that way she stood with her right foot turned out slightly.

What could possibly have led Paige's sister to that life? What would make her turn on Paige like that?

"Josh?" Caleb snapped his fingers in front of my face, bringing me back to the present. "Do you think this is Paige?"

It took a Herculean effort to force my lips to form the words. "Yes, that's her."

"Well, add this to her story. She didn't just stab some random biker; she slit their leader's throat. It explains why she thinks someone's after her." He slid his eyes sideways at me. "They are. Having the Hell Dogs trying to kill you would scare a grown man." He turned the screen back and buried himself in the deep recesses of the web.

"Whisper Cove has never had problems like that." I turned my tired eyes to him. "She is safe here, right?" We tended to be isolated from most big city problems. Strangers would be obvious. Odd behaviors stuck out like a sore thumb. My mind slid back to lunch at Avery's bar. I remembered the two men coming in while we were there that day over a month ago. Were they Hell Dogs?

"Mmmmh," Caleb was off in his own world, fingers flying across the keyboard.

"So what do we do?"

"Didn't you go to UMaine with that guy in the FBI?" he asked.

"Ryder?" I nodded. "Haven't talked to him in years, though."

"Mmmmmh. We need more information. They've updated their servers, and I'm having some trouble getting in."

I stared sternly at the screen. "You can't access it?"

"No, I'll get in. It's just gonna take a little effort."

"Okay." I pushed back from the bar, standing and shifting from one foot to the other. Sitting there with Caleb wasn't going to do any good. I needed to go find Logan. He knew Ryder better than I did. We needed a view into that database if we were going to find out who was coming for Paige.

~

I checked the time on my phone. There were only few minutes before I was due to open the clinic. Life continued no matter what dangers Paige faced. I had two well puppy exams, a rabbit who'd stopped eating, and a cat overdue with a litter of kittens.

Paige was going to take Jentil to see Ma and Daisy. It was part of an effort to reunite him with his brothers and sisters now that he was strong enough to go home. She would be okay, but I needed to find Logan before I opened. My stomach burned from the stress. How was I going to take care of Paige and the four-legged residents of Whisper Cove at the same time?

My long legs took me across the street to Logan's office. I nodded at the deputies gathered around the coffee pot and waved at his secretary before wandering straight into his inner sanctum.

"Josh," he nodded when he saw me, "is something wrong?"

"Does something have to be wrong for me to come see you?"

He rolled his eyes and looked down his nose at me. "For you to get out of the clinic and walk into the station, yes. Is Paige okay?"

"That's debatable. She's pretty shaken up since her memory came back. She needed some puppy therapy, so she's taking Jentil to see Daisy and the rest of the litter. You can't be unhappy surrounded by a dozen fat golden puppies."

He set his pencil down on top of the tall stack of reports he was reviewing. He'd complained enough that I knew it wasn't just rolling stops, people running the one red light in town at 3 am, or petty theft and kid stuff. Beneath the calm façade, our little county held some dirty deep wood secrets. Mailbox baseball was a favorite among the town's few teens, but Logan's responsibilities were darker than that. He folded his hands and just looked at me.

"Fine," I said, moving another stack of files off the only other chair, so I could sit. I folded my large frame small enough to fit in the tiny metal chair. "Caleb found a picture of Paige. The FBI wants to talk to her."

"The FBI?"

I steepled my fingers over my lips and nodded. "The guy she stabbed apparently wasn't just a member but the leader of the Hell Dogs. I don't know what her sister was mixed up in, but it had to be pretty bad."

"She killed the club president?" I had his attention.

"Yeah. I think she did."

"Shit." He leaned back in his chair, rocking in place for a minute.

"Logan, have you heard of any bikers in town? In the county?"

He shook his head and leaned back in his seat. "No reports from anyone."

I moved to the edge of the chair. "About a month ago, at Avery's, I saw these two guys I didn't recognize. They had long hair, and I couldn't tell what they did for work."

"Two guys about a month ago?"

I nodded.

He stroked his fingers along his jaw. "No one's complained about a couple of guys a month ago." Logan blew a sigh out, leaned forward, and rested his elbows on his desk. "Did you just come to bring me this good news, or is there more?"

"Do you still keep in touch with Ryder? From college? Isn't he an FBI agent now? Caleb said we need to get more information on why they want to talk to Paige."

"I haven't talked to him in a while. I think he just got married. I probably have an email address somewhere, though."

"Find it. Please, Logan. We need to know what they know."

Chapter Fifteen

Paige

"Come on in!" Ma's voice carried from somewhere in the house all the way through the closed front door. "It's open!"

I turned the knob and pushed to see her smiling at me through the kitchen doorway. "You'll have to make yourself at home, Paige. I'm elbows deep in beef and onions at the moment."

"Okay." I unbuttoned my wool coat, pulled Jentil out, and carried him into the living room to a large cordoned off area where his brothers and sisters greeted him with yaps, sniffs, and kisses. Peace washed over me as I watched the wagging celebration carry on and on. Josh was right; Prozac had nothing on puppies.

"Aah, look at them." Ma appeared in the living room entry with a grin on her face, drying her hands on a kitchen towel. "You never forget where you're from, I guess."

A wave of dread washed over me. *Stop!* I'd come to feel better, and I couldn't let innocent comments put me back down in the hole. *She doesn't even know about any of that!*

"Cup of coffee?" she asked, oblivious to the emotional roller coaster I was riding.

I forced a smile and nodded. "Yes, please." She waved for me to follow her, and with one last look at the pile of puppies, I turned and trailed her.

Ma's kitchen was a whole lot like mine, only her floors were worn linoleum where ours were hardwood, her table was red Formica instead of oak, and her whole house smelled like Sunday dinner. It was only Wednesday. Still, cookies were cooling on the counter, bread dough was rising in loaf pans, and her face was weathered with love.

"Have a seat." She pulled a couple mugs down from the cupboard and poured fresh coffee into each. "Cream and sugar?"

"Yes, please." I looked around at her gingham curtains and matching accents, and for a moment, I so envied of what she had. It wasn't much. Mack and Ma lived comfortably, but not indulgently. In fact, Josh and I probably had a lot more up in the farmhouse on Seaglass Drive, but we weren't nearly as comfortable. "I love your home," I told her as she placed a mug on the table in front of me.

"Oh." She chuckled and turned back for a plate of fresh cookies. "This place is old and falling apart, just like us." She set the cookies on the table and took a seat. "You like molasses, Paige?"

"Yes. Thank you."

"Well, they're my mother's recipe, but I'm not my mother, so keep your expectations low."

I laughed and took a cookie from the plate. She'd decorated them with a sprinkle of powdered sugar, as though being fresh and homemade just wasn't enough. I bit into one and the taste of molasses and ginger filled my senses. For a moment, I felt like I'd gone home, though I couldn't recall ever having come home to molasses cookies in my life. "They're delicious."

She nodded her head and took a sip of her coffee. "I must have baked a thousand batches of them over the years. Mack just loves them. My boys always loved them too." She raised her eyebrows. "*Josh* always loved them." Then Ma shook her head. "I grew sick of eating them about twenty years ago." She turned her gray eyes to me and smiled. "Never grew tired of baking them, though."

I thought about it for a moment. "Why is that?"

She shrugged. "I never grew tired of making my boys happy, I guess."

When Ma wasn't stumbling over unmarked conversational graves, she was an easy lady to be around. She was a nurturer in every sense of the word. She wanted to feed people, care for puppies, and comfort troubled strangers like me. That afternoon, she gave me more food than Josh and I could eat and more advice than I could ever put to good use.

We moved our chat to the living room to watch the puppies play while we finished another cup of coffee. She shook her head and blew out a deep breath while she studied Jentil. "You and Josh worked a miracle on that one."

Jentil had his mouth open and his paws up, sitting like Buddha with his belly out in front of him while one of his siblings mirrored his posture. I laughed. "Yeah. He's not as big as the others, though."

"He never will be," she said, "but he's alive, and he's beautiful." She lifted her watery eyes to me. "And he wouldn't be if you two hadn't saved him." She set her hand on my knee. "He doesn't have to be like all the others to be perfect."

As I watched the chubby puppy play and wag and yap, I knew she was right. Maybe things didn't have to be the same. Maybe people didn't have to be perfect. Maybe it was okay to have scars and skeletons and be loved by someone who has neither.

Maybe you need a reality check.

Jentil came to the side of the crate, stood up on his hind

legs, and yapped for my attention. I waved to him with the tip of my finger and smiled. "Are you having fun?"

"He's become quite attached to you," she said. "You must have a strong motherly instinct."

"Me?" I smiled and tilted my head at the puppy. "Maybe."

She set a light hand on my arm. "I don't mean to pry, but do you and Josh have any plans together?"

I watched Jentil's little tail wag, and sadness swept over me like an icy cold breeze. I shook my head. "I'll probably be heading home soon."

"Where's home?" Ma wasn't trying to be nosey. It was a reasonable question that any reasonable person would be able to answer. My life, however, wasn't reasonable. Rather than lie, I kept my mouth shut. Wise and kind as she was, Ma didn't pry.

Still, I felt like I had to offer *some* explanation. "Whisper Cove is lovely. I just don't think I fit in here. You've all been so nice to me, but… my life is very complicated. I wouldn't be good for Josh in the long run." I shrugged. "And it wouldn't be good for me." I took a deep breath and fought back tears. "It's better for both of us if I move on soon."

The phone rang out in the kitchen, and Ma slowly came to her feet. "I wonder who that could be."

"Maybe it's Josh. Maybe Chloe had her baby." I knew I shouldn't have been thinking about babies and enduring love, but I couldn't help it. Ma's house was a monument to both those things.

"Paige," she said from the living room doorway, "Avery's on the phone for you. She sounds like she's in a hurry."

I followed Ma back to the kitchen and picked the phone up off the counter. "Hello?"

"Paige! Thank God! You have to call Josh! You have to get somewhere safe!"

All the calm Ma and the puppies had given to me instantly turned to terror. "What do you mean?"

"I've called everywhere looking for you! You didn't answer your phone!"

I looked down at my short wool skirt and realized it didn't have any pockets. My phone was probably still in my jacket. "I'm sorry, Avery. What's going on?"

"There were guys here. Three of them. They came in on Harleys and ordered cheap beers. They asked me if I knew a woman named Paige. They showed me your picture!"

"Oh my God," I whispered. The fear I'd felt that first night, the urgent need to run, flooded my senses once again. "Oh my God!"

"I went over to the clinic to tell Josh, but he was already gone for the day. When I tried to call him, I could hear his cell phone ringing inside his office." The worry in her voice only added to my panic. "You need to get somewhere safe! Does Josh have a gun in the house?"

"Yes." My voice was barely more than a breath.

"Go home. Lock the doors. Get the gun. Don't let anyone in unless it's Josh, okay?! I'm gonna tell Caleb and Logan." She paused only long enough to take a breath and shout, "Go now!"

The line clicked and the call ended. I hung the phone up on the wall and turned around. "I have to go," I told Ma. I was too upset to even come up with an excuse.

"Is everything okay?"

Shaking my head, I began to cry. "No. No, it's not okay."

"Is there anything I can do to help?"

I wiped my tears with the back of my hand, but the stream never stopped. "Um… can you keep Jentil?"

"Of course, dear."

"I'll come back for him tonight." I took my wool coat from the back of the kitchen chair and put my arms in the sleeve. Reaching into my pockets, I found the Mustang's keys on the right and my phone on the left—with the ringer turned off.

"Don't you worry about him," she said. "He'll be fine with his family."

"Okay," I sniveled on my way to the door. "I'm really sorry."

"Nonsense." She rubbed my back firmly.

I looked into the living room at the tangle of happy puppies. There in the middle, the small one was Jentil. "I love you, Jentil," I said. As I rushed out the door and down the steps to the car, I had the horrible sense I'd never see him again.

Josh

"Dammit," I muttered to myself as I slid out of the truck at the gas station, patting my packets. No cell phone. I leaned back in and searched first underneath and then between the seats. Sifting through the detritus of my life, I found a half-empty box of latex gloves, two paper coffee cups, a broken ink pen, and the stethoscope I had already replaced a year ago— but no cell phone.

"Stupid, Josh." *I must have left it back at the clinic.* I sighed, I really didn't want to go back, but it looked like I was going to have to. I couldn't be unreachable all night.

I rolled my shoulders to shake off some of the stress and slid my credit card into the gas pump. With the nozzle in the truck, I leaned back against the door as the hungry tank slurped down gallon after gallon. Looking down at my boots, I shook my head at my stupidity. *You have no business getting involved with anyone. You can barely keep track of yourself.*

As I stood there sulking against the truck, I idly looked around the old gas station. The antique pumps gleamed in contrast to the smattering of newer vehicles driving in and out. Triplets was an odd blend of the past and the future that came together in a strange but functional present. It managed to hold all our memories, meet all our needs, and still welcome the inevitable changes of our future. It was exactly what every country store should be.

As the cavernous tank took in more and more fuel, a sound like rolling thunder filled the parking lot. I turned my head toward the road just as a group of bikers careened in. Maybe a dozen or so steel and chrome machines filled every available space in the lot. My blood ran cold as I squinted to read the writing on their leathers. "Hell Dogs. Williston." Everything in my stomach rose to my throat.

My grip on the nozzle slackened, and the whoosh of the pumping gas trickled to a stop. I reflexively reached in my pocket for my phone, cursing again when I remembered it wasn't there. "Dammit!"

Fumbling, I put the nozzle back onto the pump and struggled to screw the gas cap back into the truck. It took me two tries before I got the threads lined up. The pump beeped as it completed the transaction, and I tore the receipt in half as I rushed to rip it off the printer. Resisting the urge to sprint, which would have drawn attention, I strolled around the truck, and launched myself into the driver's seat. Turning the ignition switch, I drew a calming breath and cleared my head as the engine roared to life.

I accidentally peeled out of the parking lot, kicking up gravel as I flew back to town. I needed to find Paige. I needed to tell Logan. *Shit! What if I'm too late? What if they've already found her?!*

I took the hills at high speed, my stomach lurching and dropping as I went up and down, covering the ten miles in half the time it normally took me. *She's probably still at Ma's,* I thought, practically chewing a hole through my lip. *They'd never find her there. They don't know the Mustang.* Then I thought again. *What if word got to her? What if she went back to the house… alone?*

I shivered at that thought, the image too gruesome to

dwell on. The truck slid to a stop in a cloud of gravel dust, and I raced to the clinic door, my hands shaking so badly I could barely get the key into the lock. When it finally slid home, I was in and out in seconds, my precious cell phone clutched in my hand.

I frantically dialed Paige, my heart hammering in my chest as I waited for her to answer. Her voice mail picked up. "Please leave a message!" Her sunny voice was followed with an excruciating *beeeep!*

"Goddammit!" I threw the phone down on the seat. "Where the hell are you?!"

Home. She must be home. God, I hoped so. Back on the road, I frantically called Logan, filling him in on what I'd seen. Then, with my hopeful heart in my throat, I asked, "Have you seen her around anywhere?"

"Nope." I could hear him shuffling through papers. "But if I run into her on my rounds, I promise to keep her safe."

"Thanks, Logan."

Avery was next on my speed dial. "Josh?!"

"Avery! Thank God! Is Paige with you?!"

"No! She just left Ma's. She's on her way home. Josh, they're here. The Hell Dogs are *here!*"

"I know. I just saw them at the gas station. They were in the bar?"

"Three of them. I tried to call you, but you didn't answer. Paige didn't answer, either, but Caleb told me she was at Ma's, so I tracked her down there."

"She's still not answering her phone, Avery!"

"She's heading home, Josh. She should be there in just a few minutes."

"Thank God. Avery, I'm headed there now. If anything else happens, call me right away."

"Okay."

"Avery, if she calls you, tell her to call me right away. Right?"

“Right.” She paused. “Good luck, Josh.”

“Thank you.”

I could only pray Paige was safe at the house when I got there. I wasn’t used to worrying about another person like this. I didn’t know what I would do if I lost her.

Chapter Sixteen

Paige

There must be back roads into Canada. I turned into the driveway, and the Mustang rumbled along the gravel. *The only way south is through New Hampshire. That's a bottleneck. They might be waiting for me there. Shit!*

I parked the car and flew up the steps. The front door was unlocked and swung open easily at the turn of the knob. This time, *I'd* left it unlocked.

Damnit, Paige! You're as bad as Josh!

I hesitated before stepping into the house, acutely aware that anyone could be waiting anywhere inside to attack me—in a closet, under a bed, around any corner. "Get the gun." I muttered. "Get the gun, get some cash, and run." Steeling my nerves, I repeated the words over and over and forced myself forward. "Get the gun, get some cash, and run. Get the gun, get some cash, and run."

Leaving the door open behind me in case I needed to make a escape, I ran to the broom closet for Josh's shotgun. Next to it was a box of ammunition, so I grabbed that too. I carried it all to the kitchen table, staring at the weaponry like it was alien technology. I'd never even held a gun before, let alone loaded one. I didn't have time to sit down and figure it out, but Josh didn't keep it loaded.

I opened the box of shells, my hands trembling so hard nearly half of them spilled out onto the floor. Finally catching a grasp on one, I carried them both to the stairs, and tried to figure it out as I climbed the steps. There was a slot on the right hand side that roughly matched the shape of the shell, so I shoved it in and it fit. It rattled around loose inside until I remembered I'd seen heroes in movies always sliding something down the barrel before they shot it. There was only one piece that could be, so I slid it along the length and heard the shell snap into place.

"Money, money, money," I whispered, moving at a frantic pace. I didn't want to steal from Josh—not again—but I also didn't want him to get killed on my behalf. There was no way I was getting to Canada or the New Hampshire border without gas money, and until I was far away from him, his life would be at risk.

In the closet where Josh's mother's clothes still hung, I'd run into a small box with a short stack of cash hidden inside. It wasn't much, maybe two hundred dollars, but it was enough to get the hell out of town. I could figure the rest out on the road.

I pocketed the cash and looked down at myself. It was cold out and a wool skirt and tights wasn't the most practical 'on the lam' ensemble. "It will take thirty seconds to throw some clothes in a bag," I muttered. Then, making my way back to Josh's room, where my own clothes filled the closet, I passed a framed photo of Josh and me that I'd hung on the wall only a couple weeks earlier. In it, I was holding Jentil, kissing his furry little head while Josh kissed my cheek. Avery had taken it down at the pub and given it to us as a gift. My heart broke when I thought of leaving it behind. With my free hand, I tore it from the wall and carried it into the bedroom.

There, I looked out the window, relieved to see the Mustang was still the only car in the driveway. "You'll hear them, Paige. Motorcycles are loud. They can't sneak up on you." I took a breath, tried to slow my heart, and kept moving.

Packing was slower with a shotgun in one hand, but I still managed to get Josh's suitcase onto the bed, throw the top open, and set the picture inside. I grabbed a handful of panties from the top dresser drawer, some socks, and a couple pairs of jeans from the middle. I kept my shirts and blouses in the closet. Turning to fetch them, I came face-to-face with the shape of a tall man standing in bedroom doorway.

Without a word, I raised the shotgun, pointed at the form, and pulled the trigger.

Josh

"Hey! Hey! Wait! It's me!" My hands flew up as I took a step forward, trying to knock the shotgun to the side. Nothing like walking in on your girlfriend trying to shoot you.

Click!

Her eyes were blind with panic, and she pulled the trigger again, just as I dove to the side while reaching for the barrel.

"Oh my God!" She heard my voice and came out of her fear fugue. Dropping the gun like it was hot, she stared up at me as it bounced on the stock and came to rest at her feet with a clatter. "I almost shot you!" She fell to her knees next to me where I had landed on the hardwood when I dove for my life. I really *was* getting too old for this.

"Shhh… shhh…" I tried to stop her as her shaky hands roamed all over me in search of holes. "You didn't. It's okay. You forgot to take the safety off. Paige…" Tears streamed down her face as her eyes scoured my body. "PAIGE!" Her eyes flicked up. "I'm fine. Really."

"I can't do this. I just can't do this anymore. It's not safe."

She rambled, the words tumbling from her lips in a rush. "I love you, I love this town, and I'm poison. They're after me. I brought them here to Whisper Cove, to you. This isn't right." She stood, one shaky hand brushing her hair from her face, and turned back to my old suitcase. A little worn, a little scuffed, a little dusty from being stored for so long, it now sat open on the bed, clothes hanging half in and out as she ran around gathering what little she owned, shoving it all haphazardly inside.

"You saw them?" I grabbed the footboard and pulled myself back up on my feet. "The bikers?"

"No, but Avery called me." She turned her back on me, tossing a few more things into the case before closing the lid and zipping it shut. "I need to go now. Before anything bad happens, I need to get far away from this place."

"They don't know where you are. You're still safe here." I walked up behind her, cocooning her. I placed one arm around her middle and set my other hand over hers, stilling it, stopping her chaotic frenzy. She leaned back into me for a moment, her free arm coming down to settle on mine. "Call Logan," I whispered in her ear. "He'll tell you. It's better to be here where we can protect you than out there where anything could happen."

She shook her head. "I just can't. I would never forgive myself if anything happened to you… or to anyone else here."

"Paige, please don't go."

DING!

My phone buzzed at the arrival of a new message. I stood perfectly still, keeping her in a prison of my embrace.

DING!

She stiffened, twisting out of my arms and grabbing the suitcase. She slid it off the bed and let it land upright on the floor.

"Paige, wait!" I reached into my pocket to silence my cell.

"You should really get that." She pulled the handle up on

the case and rolled it toward the bedroom door. "It might be important." On her way, she crouched down and picked the shotgun up off the floor. She tucked it under her arm and walked out the bedroom door, pulling the suitcase behind her.

I had lost her.

"Nothing is more important than you!" That tenuous connection we'd felt for a moment snapped, and she was no longer listening to me. "At least let me go with you!"

"People here need you, Josh." She descended the stairs without so much as a glance back at me. "They count on you. I can't take you away from them." And with that, she reached the bottom step and walked right out the door, shutting it behind her.

"Paige, wait!" I peeked down at my phone.

A text from Avery waited for me. *BABY COMING! NOW!*

Before I could respond, another message came in from Logan. *No sign of Paige. Still looking. Call Avery. Chloe in labor.*

"Shit, Shit, SHIT!" I didn't have time for this. I had told Chloe she was too close to delivery and needed to go to Bangor this week. Like every other woman I knew, she was stubborn and refused to listen to reason.

I dialed Avery. "Josh!"

"I'm a fucking vet," I growled into the phone. "I'm not a fucking obstetrician." I stormed down the stairs to stop Paige. "Put her in the car and drive her to the hospital."

"Josh, listen—"

"No! I'm not listening. I have my own shit, Avery." My blood ran hot as I threw the front door open and stormed out on the porch.

"Josh!" Avery's voice squeaked with desperation. "Listen to me! She's not gonna make it to the hospital. I can't even get her into bed."

Then, in the background, I heard Chloe's scared, pleading voice. "Josh! Please help me!"

As I listened to her cries, I watched Paige peel out of the

long driveway, the Mustang fishtailing in the gravel, leaving nothing behind but a cloud of dust.

I stood there, staring as the car disappeared down Seaglass Drive, my heart torn from my chest. I muttered, "I'm on my way."

Chapter Seventeen

Paige

The tank was half full. That was enough to get me out of Whisper Cove and maybe all the way to Bangor if traffic was light. I paid no attention to my speed. Honestly, I didn't even know what the limit was. I could barely see the road through my tears and panic.

The drive seemed to take forever. I floored the gas up the enormous hills, thinking each time that just on the other side, I'd find the town line, but it never seemed to appear. After a while, I began to think maybe I'd already passed it without even noticing.

In the passenger seat, my phone began to vibrate, and the sound made me jump. Keeping my blurry eyes on the road, I ignored it, and after a few vibrations, it stopped. I wiped my nose, proud for having resisted the urge to answer it, but then it started again. This happened three times before I finally picked it up.

"Josh, leave me alone!" I yelled at the top of my lungs, more frightened than angry.

"You ran out on me." He sounded hurt, violated. "It was an emergency. I had to answer the message."

"Good!" I cried. "I wanted you to answer it, Josh."

"Chloe's having her baby."

My face twisted in anguish as the stream continued to flow down my cheeks. "She is?"

"Yeah! She's not going to make it to the hospital. She needs me there, Paige." He was quiet for a moment. "And I need you. Come back. Come with me."

"You really want Chloe's baby born with my mess around?"

"You're not a mess, Paige! You're a victim of a crime you had no control over!"

I shook my head. "I slit a gangster's throat, Josh. I'm not a victim."

"That was self-defense!" he shouted. "You had no choice, Paige. Everyone knows that. Even Logan knows that! If he didn't, you'd already be in jail!"

"The Hell Dogs don't know it... or they don't care. They're there, Josh. They're looking for me." I struggled around an eerily familiar sharp turn with the phone in one hand and the wheel in the other.

"Come back and we can protect you. We have guns and the law on our side, Paige. Logan can have men protect you day and night—"

"And what about you, Josh?! Who's gonna protect you while you're rescuing puppies and delivering babies? Are you going to take a couple deputies to Chloe's birth?"

"If I have to! I'll do whatever I have to, Paige. I just need you here!"

"No," I whispered, staring blankly at the road ahead.

"Paige, I don't have time for this! Chloe needs me!"

"I know," I said. "The whole town needs you, Josh. You're important."

"You're important too, Paige!" Desperation dripped from

his voice, making me wish I could hold him, comfort him. "Please come back. We'll figure this out."

I shook my head and sobbed. Rain was beginning to fall, making my already limited vision even worse. "You can't help me, Josh. You can help Chloe."

"I can help you both! Just not at the same time. Come back. Please! I don't have time to chase you right now! Let me deliver the baby, and then we'll work with Logan to figure out what comes next."

"Nothing comes next, Josh!" I screamed. "We're done!"

I rolled down the window in urgent need of air. Then I pressed, turned, and flipped every button and switch I could find on the dashboard until the wipers came on. They swept clarity across the windshield right in time to show headlights coming straight at me. I'd crossed the line and was driving into oncoming traffic.

"Holy fuck!" I grabbed the wheel with both hands, dropping the phone, and turned it all the way to the right, narrowly escaping a head-on collision with an oncoming pickup. The other vehicle blew its horn as it continued on down the road in the opposition direction.

Over the swish of the wipers, I could hear Josh's voice coming from the phone on the passenger side floor, but I couldn't make out the words. It didn't matter. There was nothing left to say.

"I'm gonna go, Josh," I yelled. "I'm in big trouble, and you don't need that. Logan doesn't need that. Chloe doesn't need that." I heard his faint shouting, but ignored it. "Whisper Cove needs you. If I stay… if you stay with me… we're both gonna end up dead." I shook my head and wept. "I don't want that. Please don't make me do that to you. I can't live with that."

I could barely hear his shouting, "Paige! Paige!"

"I love you, Josh, but this is over." Reaching down across

the passenger seat, I picked my phone up off the floor and threw it out the window before I could change my mind.

Josh

"FUCK!" Every bone in my body screamed for me to get in the truck and chase her down, to make her stop and come to her senses. But taxes and babies wait for no one, and Chloe was already two weeks overdue.

DING!

Contractions three minutes apart.

I dialed her number. "Dammit, Avery, I'm coming. Did you call the paramedics?"

"I did, but she refuses to go anywhere until you get here."

Women! This was why my relationships never lasted. Paige was the closest I had come to settling down, and now that was blowing up in my face. They really were from a different planet. *Why they hell is Chloe waiting for me?* I delivered babies with a calf pulling rope. *What woman in her right mind wants me in the delivery room?*

And Paige—what the hell was I going to do about Paige? I couldn't take care of the whole town and Paige's drama at the same time. I also couldn't let her go barreling out of town at top speed with a homicidal motorcycle gang hot on her heels. I needed help.

So I dialed the one person I knew she wouldn't want me to turn to.

"Josh Dalton," his hard voice answered.

"Logan. Thank God." He'd picked up almost before the first ring. "All hell's breaking loose."

"You found Paige?"

"She was at the house, but she left. I couldn't talk any sense into her. I can't go after her, Logan. Chloe's in labor.

The baby will be here any minute." I glanced at my watch and realized I needed to hurry. Time was passing fast.

"Well, shit." I could picture the look on his face. Logan had a mysterious history, and like Caleb, he'd seen and done dark stuff in the Marines. I didn't know if he could handle the gang, but I knew he stood a better chance than I did. "You know, I *am* an officer of the law, Josh."

"I know." I stormed out the front door and raced down the steps to the truck.

He breathed in through his teeth, deliberately taunting me. "I may be of *some* use in a situation like this."

"Damnit, Logan, I tried! She wouldn't listen to me." I climbed behind the wheel and started the engine. "She's out of her fucking mind with panic." I hesitated for a moment, then took a breath and let it out. "She tried to shoot me."

The line fell quiet for a moment. "What's that?"

I backed down my driveway without even looking. "She had my shotgun. She mistook me for one of the bikers and tried to shoot me."

"She actually pulled the trigger?"

I shook my head as I took off down the road. "She doesn't know anything about guns, and she forgot the safety was on."

"Where's the gun now?" His voice was calm, but I knew he was about to take action.

I sighed. "She took it."

"You gave an unstable individual your car and your gun?"

"No! I didn't give them to her! She just took them and left!"

I could almost hear him nod. "Okay. I'm on this." I heard him turn his mouth from the phone and shout orders at his deputies. "Close the roads, set up roadblocks, no one leaves town. Everyone checks in every 15 minutes. Wear your vests. I don't care how hot they are. Someone send a message to Ryder West at the FBI. Let him know we've spotted their BOLO." Drill Sergeant Fox had appeared, and his team would respond. Then his voice was back on the phone with me. "Have you spoken to Avery?"

"Avery is so far up my ass right now I'm surprised it's not her voice coming from my lips."

"You go take care of Chloe," he said. "Let me do my job."

"Logan, please, I'm begging you—don't let anything happen to Paige." I bit my lip and white-knuckled the wheel. "Whatever you gotta do, just keep her safe."

There was silence on the other end of the line for a moment. "You do your job, Josh, and I'll do mine."

We ended the call right as I came upon the big farmhouse at Beach Rose Crossing.

"Please God, don't let anything go wrong with this baby."

Chapter Eighteen

Paige

It seemed like I'd been driving forever when I finally saw the faded, cracked sign through the waves of rain on my windshield. "Whisper Cove - We Wish You Would Stay!" I drove my foot down on the gas pedal, eager to put the town and Josh behind me once and for all.

Soon the sign was so close I could see the needles of the pine trees painted beneath the words. I took a deep breath, ready to reach escape velocity. I could almost feel the air change around me when the red and blue lights began flashing behind me.

"Fuck!" My foot lingered on the gas pedal. I could tell from the lights that it was a Sheriff's vehicle. I doubted it was a deputy. He certainly wouldn't have sent one after me. If Logan was going to take me down, he was going to do it himself.

As I kept going, my eye on the town line, I could see Logan closing the distance between us. *Keep driving!* I wondered if he'd really come after me, if he'd follow me beyond the boundaries of Whisper Cove. *If I don't stop, will he follow me until*

I run out of gas? A vision crossed my mind of the Mustang crawling to a pathetic stop miles down the road with Logan pulling up behind me. *If I run, will he chase me on foot?* I looked down at my inch-high Mary Janes and realized I didn't stand a chance.

Still, I kept going, past the town line, and watched in the rearview to see what Logan would do. As if he could read my mind, he raised his hand and waved. Knowing I'd just eventually sputter out on the side of the rural route, I put my right turn signal on and lifted my foot off the gas. "Asshole."

On the rainy shoulder, I waited in the car for Logan's tall form to emerge, but it didn't. Instead, a speaker on top of his car crackled to life. "Driver! Turn the car off!"

"Driver?" I rolled my eyes, but followed his command.

"Driver! Roll the window down and drop the keys on the ground!"

"What?"

As though he could hear me, he said it again. "Driver! Roll the window down and drop the keys on the ground."

You're really gonna make a thing out of this, aren't you Logan?

"Driver, roll—"

Before he could repeat himself a third time, I pulled the keys from the switch and dropped them out the window. It was still raining, and my arm was soon covered in droplets that gathered on the sleeve of my wool coat. I heard a door open behind me and watched in the rearview as Logan stepped out in his tan and brown all-weather gear. He shut the door to his cruiser and immediately pulled the gun from his holster.

"What the hell?"

"Driver," Logan shouted, his gun pointed at my door, "put both hands out the car window."

"Logan?!" I shouted. My heart pounded. He *had* to recognize Josh's car, didn't he? *Does he even know it's me?*

"Paige Carlisle, put your hands out the window where I can see them!" He took a cautious step forward, pointing the gun directly at my head. "I know you have the shotgun, Paige. Put your hands out the window and don't do anything stupid."

"For God's sake, Logan," I muttered. I pulled the handle and the door popped open.

"Paige!" Logan's voice boomed, mean and ugly. "I *will* shoot you! I am *not* Josh! I do *not* deliver babies!"

"Okay!" I shouted. The door sat barely ajar and I stuck my hands out through the open window. *Josh must have called him. He can have the gun, but I'm not going back.*

"Keep your hands outside the vehicle!" Logan slowly made his way across the back of the car, keeping his gun aimed at me all the way. He came around to the passenger side, and I watched as he opened the door and grabbed the shotgun from the floor. He stepped away from the car and returned to his cruiser with the one gun pointed at me and the other pointed at the ground. Behind me, I heard the action of the shotgun and then the clinking of the shell hitting the pavement.

A moment later, he was right back at my side, his handgun still drawn. "With one hand, I want you to push the door all the way open."

"You can take the gun off me, Logan. I'm not dangerous."

"Do it, Paige!" I sighed loudly to make my annoyance clear. "Do it!"

I pushed the door open with one hand, and then made the bold move of stepping out of the vehicle.

"Stop!" he shouted in his best cop voice, but I didn't comply. I was beginning to think being shot by Logan was a better fate than being chased down and tortured to death by the Hell Dogs. "Put your hands in the air!" I did, and Logan moved in fast, pulling the cuffs from his belt, grabbing my right arm, and twisting it behind my back.

"Take it easy, Logan. You know I'm not gonna hurt you."

"You're not, huh? You slit one guy's throat, and you tried

to shoot one of my best friends today." He locked one cuff around my right wrist—*snap*—and then pulled my left arm behind my back. "You're speeding down the road, failing to comply with instructions." *Snap.* "Sounds erratic to me."

"I can't believe you're putting me in cuffs."

"Paige Carlisle, I am placing you under arrest for suspicion of grand larceny."

My jaw dropped, and I stared at him in utter disbelief. "They were going to kill me, Logan! You know I had to take that truck!"

"This Mustang has been reported stolen by Dr. Joshua Dalton."

I glared and shook my head. "Bullshit."

"I am also placing you under arrest for suspicion of capital murder."

I gasped. "What?! You said yourself that was self-defense!"

"You have the right to remain silent," he said. "Anything you say—"

"You said you were my friend, Logan!" I cried. "You said I could trust you."

"Well," he said. "I guess you're not the only liar in town."

Josh

I rolled my shoulders, straightening up and stretching the kinks out of my back as I set my medicine bag on the living room floor. It seemed like forever since I'd walked out the door thirteen hours ago to go deliver Chloe's baby. Like all first babies, the little bugger took forever, but after 16 hours in labor, she finally delivered a healthy baby boy. Mom and baby were then safely transported to the nearest hospital two hours away, and both were doing fine.

As I stood in the empty kitchen, the old farmhouse seemed

cavernous. I never realized how big and empty it was until Jentil and Paige blew into my life. And then they were gone. Ma reported Jentil was playing happily, eating, pooping, and making friends. Still small, but so spunky he was holding his own among his larger siblings.

I kicked off my boots, leaving them where they lay in the middle of the floor. There was no one around to trip over them or complain about my mess. My shirt came next. I dropped it on the back of a kitchen chair, unbuttoning my jeans and leaving them loose as I trudged up the stairs.

Paige saw the beauty in the old house. The aged books with inscriptions from my ancestors, the bannister my mother lovingly polished every Sunday like clockwork, the built in shelves my father had spent every night out in his wood shop crafting to her exact specifications to fit in the funny shaped space under the stairs—Paige listened to all those stories and treasured that history almost as much as I did. But Paige was gone.

Purple streaks crept across the sky as I closed the blinds, blocking out the coming day, and finally stripped off my pants. I walked naked into the bathroom to stand under the hot shower, and it hit me that Paige hadn't been there first to use up all the hot water, leaving me to dance in a cold morning shower. I should have been happier about that.

I missed her. I missed her beautiful voice singing in the shower. I missed her doting love for Jentil. I even missed the way she left the toothpaste all twisted and misshapen, sitting by the faucet with the cap off. Without her, the house was so empty it seemed to echo, every sound coming back to me with the message that I really was all alone.

Less than an hour into the delivery, Logan had reported back that he'd caught up with Paige, and she was tucked up safe in a cell. I didn't get all the details, but he gave me the impression she went willingly. *Good. At least she doesn't know I told him to do whatever it took to keep her from leaving.*

I grabbed a pen from the nightstand. I needed to call Owen, but it was too late… or too early. His cousin Ryder was an FBI agent, and I wanted Owen to get his advice. Owen was a good lawyer, but I doubted he had much experience with extradition and capital murder cases. Paige was going to need the best to beat the theft and murder charges, no matter how innocent she was. I hated to say it, but I didn't trust her life in the hands of a public defender. I didn't know if this mess involved the FBI, but if it did she'd need someone truly connected on her side like Ryder. As soon as I woke up, I would go into town, find Owen, and call Ryder.

Still wet from the shower, I fell into bed. The sheets still smelled of Paige's shampoo and the puppy. I slept, dreaming of the life we could have had.

Chapter Nineteen

Paige

The security door slid open. Lying on my side with my arm over my eyes, I could just see the bottom inch of Logan's shiny leather boots. They stopped outside the bars of my cell, and he cleared his throat. "I brought you a muffin and a cup of coffee."

"Keep it," I croaked, my throat raw from crying all night. "I want my phone call and my lawyer."

The sound of metal chair legs dragging across concrete filled the echoing cells. The keys on his belt jangled as he sat down. I heard a paper bag crumpling and the sound of a lid popping off. He slurped a sip. "Aaah… that's some good coffee, Paige."

"Choke on it, Logan."

"Yup." He set his cup down on the floor. "I had a feeling you'd be like that."

"You should buy a crystal ball and charge by the hour." I sat up and took a moment to glare at him.

"You were never gonna make it out of Maine alive, Paige."

"We'll never know now, will we?"

He looked down at his coffee and nodded. "I know. We had reports from Kittery to Rangely to Jackman to Fort Kent—"

"I don't know where any of those places are."

"And that's one of the reasons you'd be dead right now if I hadn't brought you in."

"This is a lot better than dead, isn't it?" I pushed myself off the steel bunk and paced around my cell like a trapped animal. "Stuck in a cage, facing multiple charges, possible death." I stopped and looked at him, suddenly worried. "Is North Dakota a lethal injection state, or do they use the electric chair there?"

He took another sip of coffee and shook his head. "There's no death penalty in North Dakota, not that it would matter to *you* for a while. The way things stand, you're probably not gonna make it back to face charges in Williston for a while."

"You let me think I was facing the death penalty—" I stopped in my tracks and glared at him. "What do you mean I'm not gonna make it back to Williston?"

"Well, not in the immediate foreseeable future." He took a bite of his muffin and washed it down with a swig of coffee.

I hadn't thought it possible for my situation to get worse, but looking a Logan's smug face, I had a sick feeling it was about to. "And why is that?"

"You're property of the FBI, Paige Elizabeth Carlisle."

I shook my head. "What?"

"Murder's one thing. Human trafficking's another matter entirely."

"Human trafficking?!" I charged toward him and grabbed the bars with both hands, but Logan didn't even flinch. "I was trying to save my sister from human trafficking!"

"Mmmhmmm." He reached down, picked a file up off the concrete floor, and gave it a quick once over. "That would be the sister you stabbed in the heart when she refused to return to Nebraska with you?"

"What?!"

He looked down at the file again, and I could have sworn he was trying to hold back a smile. "The FBI suspects you went to the Wrong Way Tavern in Williston that night for the purpose of collecting Melody Grant with the intention of transporting her to Nebraska—"

I nodded. "I did. That's exactly why I went there. I told you that."

"—at which time you planned to force Miss Grant to engage in prostitution against her will."

I stepped back from the bars, my ears ringing, my eyes wide with shock. "You're crazy. Logan, you know I didn't do that. You know I'm innocent."

He sipped his coffee and nodded. "It doesn't matter what I think. The FBI is unconvinced."

Throwing my hands in the air, I looked up at concrete ceiling. "I've never even had a speeding ticket!"

"Mmmm…" He set his coffee down. "That reminds me—I need to write you up for goin' ninety in a fifty-five."

I closed my eyes and a demented smile spread across my lips. Everything kept getting worse, and I didn't know how to make it stop.

He closed the file with a *snap!* "Anyway, I'm sure the nice FBI agent will explain all that to you in the interview."

"I can't believe this." Through teary eyes, I looked the bastard up and down. "You're supposed to be Josh's friend. How does he not know what an evil piece of shit you are?"

He sniffed calmly. "Maybe Josh isn't such a great judge of character."

I stared him dead in his cold eyes. "You're a horrible person."

Logan nodded and came to his feet, pushing the metal

folding chair back away from my cell. "Probably, but you're a lucky girl."

I laughed. "How do you figure that?"

"Well, if you weren't suspected of engaging in human trafficking, this wouldn't be in the hands of the FBI. You'd already be on your way back to Williston to stand trial for the murder of Walter King Riley, aka Pitbull King, and I promise you, Paige, if you go back there in handcuffs, you'll leave prison in a body bag… *if* you even make it to prison." He yawned, lifted up on his toes, and stretched his long arms over his head, making himself look about ten feet tall. Then he settled back down on his heels with a groan. "My guess is you'd get beat to death in jail when the warden stuck you in general population, and all the guards would look the other way. You'd never even make it to trial." He chuckled. "Isn't that funny? Your dead prostitute sister just saved your life."

I kept my mouth shut and watched him as the depths of my troubles became clearer to me.

"I read somewhere that the FBI's been working on bringing down the Hell Dogs for a long time. They got some sort of human trafficking case they're building." He took another sip of coffee and shrugged. "Could be they're looking for witnesses. Could be if you cooperated and promised to help them put these guys behind bars, the FBI would be a lot more concerned about your personal safety."

He bent over and placed the paper bakery bag and the second cup of coffee on the floor just outside my cell, within my reach. "You have a good breakfast, Paige. Do some thinkin'. It's good for the digestion."

Josh

My boots squeaked on the worn linoleum as I made a beeline for Logan's office. "Where is she?"

Behind his desk, he leaned back in his chair. "In a cell."

"Still?! Why?!"

Logan laced his fingers behind his neck and propped his boots up on his desk, "You told me to do whatever it took."

I clenched my fists and scowled. "I thought you'd try nice first."

"You shouldn't assume a thing like that, Josh." He shook his head. "Nah, nice takes too much time. She crossed the city limits going about ninety miles an hour, and the situation became more urgent."

I slapped my hands down on his desk and leaned a hard glare at him. "So what's she doing in a cell?"

All around us, busy men and women in uniform stopped what they were doing and turned toward us with their hands on their holsters. Logan raised his palm, a quiet signal for everyone to stand down, and they all resumed their work.

Dropping his feet back down to the floor, he leaned toward me across the desk and lowered his voice. "I saw she was in your dad's old Mustang. I know how you love that car, so I figured it would be easier to just arrest her for stealing it than to convince her to voluntarily come back to the station with me."

"That's fucking bullshit, Logan. You know I didn't report it stolen. You know I wouldn't do that to her."

Logan's hands flew up in the air. "You said, 'whatever it takes.'"

I paced back and forth across his office floor. "Not that."

He nodded. "That's half her problem, Josh. She's been in a world of shit without any direction for too damned long."

Rage burned inside me. If we'd have been anywhere else, I would have knocked his teeth out, but assaulting him when we were surrounded by deputies would only get me arrested, and then I wouldn't be any help to Paige. So I took a step back and resisted the urge to punch the smug clean from his face. "Where is she? I need to talk to her now!"

He waved a lazy hand at me as he took a long sip of his coffee, making a face as the acrid swill hit his tongue. "Just head to the back. It's open. She's in the only occupied cell. Maybe she's come to her senses by now. Maybe she'll be a little more reasonable."

I gave him a cold stare, hoping he knew I planned to settle the score with him later. Then I turned on one booted heel and went to find Paige. She had to understand this was not what I wanted.

"Paige!" I called, entering the cell area. "Honey? Are you okay?"

"Fuck you!" She spat out, slamming into the cell bars. "How could you have told Logan I stole your car!" Her eyes blazed as her hands gripped the cold metal so tight her knuckles turned white. I took a step back from her rage. Her body vibrated with anger as she eyed me through hateful slits.

"I swear I never told him to do that. You have to believe me." How could everything have gone so horribly wrong? Just yesterday, I'd woken up to a naked, angelic Paige wrapped around me, her hand stroking between my legs, begging me to make love to her. Now she looked like she'd rip me apart if there weren't steel bars between us. "I love you, Paige. I didn't want you to leave, but I didn't want you in jail either."

She closed her eyes and shook her head. "It doesn't matter, Josh," she whispered, her anger suddenly gone. "Nothing matters anymore."

"What are you talking about? Of course it matters." Braving her wrath, I stepped forward and wrapped my hands around hers, which still gripped the bars. "Whatever bail is, I'll post it. I just need to talk to Owen and make arrangements."

"It's too late, Josh." She released her death grip on the

bars, pulled her hands from mine, and took a few steps back. "There's no bail for me. The stolen car doesn't matter."

I shook my head and blinked. "Why?"

"Because I'm only in Logan's custody until the FBI gets here. Then I'm being taken—" She laughed and tears fell from the corners of her eyes. "Christ, I don't even know where they're taking me."

"Why the hell does the FBI want—"

"Human trafficking." She wiped her nose with the back of her arm and nodded with her hands on her hips.

"What?"

"Apparently, the whole reason I killed Wally the Pitbull King and stabbed my sister in the heart, is because I'd planned to abduct her, haul her back to Nebraska, and pimp her out against her will."

I sat down in the metal folding chair outside her cell and wrinkled my brow as I thought through those words. "Paige, what the hell are you talking about?"

"I don't know." She sat down on her steel cot and combed her fingers through her hair. "Ask Logan. He says it's all on the FBI, but I know he's got a hand in this." She lifted her eyes to mine. "He told me I was lucky."

"Lucky? What the hell does that mean?"

"I think he's helping the FBI frame me."

My jaw dropped. When I'd put the situation in Logan's hands, I'd had no idea just how far he would let things go. "That's crazy."

She shrugged. "He's your friend, not mine."

I stared down at the floor. "I don't understand why he would do that to you… or to me."

"I think he's crazy," she said. Then she shook her head and her tired blond waves sagged around her face. "Or he's an evil genius. I don't know."

I took a deep breath and scrubbed my hands over my face. "What does Owen think?"

She lay down on her side and rested her soft cheek against the hard metal. "I don't know. Logan won't let me see a lawyer or make a phone call."

"What?!" My face burned with anger. I pulled my phone from my pocket. "I'll call Owen right now."

"Josh?" Her voice was thin and weak. I looked up from my phone to see her lying there with her eyes shut. "Logan says if I don't go with the FBI, I'll be extradited back to North Dakota, and I'll be killed in jail before I can even stand trial." She opened her eyes and stared straight at me. "Do you think he's right?"

"Logan said that?"

She nodded. "He says if I agree to go back to North Dakota and testify for the FBI, they'll put me in protective custody and the Hell Dogs won't be able to get to me."

"No…" My voice cracked and I buried my head in my hands so she couldn't see the pain and panic on my face. "You can't leave, Paige."

Her lip trembled. "I don't have a choice."

"I'll get you out of here." I looked around at the concrete and steel with no idea how to deliver on that promise. "I'll make Logan let you out, and we'll leave here."

"They'll find us. Either the cops or the FBI or the gang—someone will find us."

"Not if we change our names. We can even take Jentil with us." It might have been a crazy plan, but I was desperate, and it was all I had.

"Josh, honey." She stood up and walked back to the bars, reaching through them to take my hand. Her cold fingers wrapped around mine. "For weeks, I didn't have a name. I wondered every minute, every day who I was. All I knew was fear. Then suddenly, it all came back. I remembered my whole life—the good and the bad." She squeezed my hand. "I have a name, Josh. Paige Elizabeth Carlisle—that's me. That's my name. It's who I am." Her face hardened with the most beautiful resolve. "I won't let the Hell Dogs take my name from me. If I have to go back with the FBI and testify to put them all behind bars and clear my name, I will. I have to. For me." She sniffed and ducked her head, releasing my hand. "I won't be any good to you if I don't."

I sucked in a shaky breath and lifted my hand to her porcelain cheek. "Oh God, Paige, you are breaking my heart." She kissed my hand and stepped back, leaving me gripping the bars, wishing I could tear them apart, rip them from the cement walls and floor.

She looked up from under her thick lashes, her green eyes begging me to believe in her, to stand by her. "Come with me?"

"Jesus…" I winced at the feeling of being torn apart inside. "I want to, but I can't leave my practice."

She nodded. "Or Whisper Cove."

The tears began to fall from my eyes, and she just stood there, silently staring at me. I wanted to deny it, to tell her I'd go anywhere with her, do anything to help her, but I couldn't. And in that moment, we both realized what a liar I was. I couldn't change my name and run away with her… I couldn't even go with her to North Dakota while she fought the hardest battle of her life.

"Look," I pleaded, "don't do anything rash. I'll figure something out."

She reached out through the bars and grabbed me with both hands, pulling me close to her.

"I mean it, Paige. Don't do *anything* yet. Don't say anything. Don't sign anything. Let me talk to Owen." Gazing into those beautiful emerald eyes, I shook my head. "I can't lose you."

She leaned forward, closed her eyes, and kissed me softly between the cold, steel bars. Then she let me go. "I loved you so much."

Chapter Twenty

Paige

Josh had friends. His friends had friends. With the notable exception of Sheriff Logan Fox, none of his friends had ever let me down. So when Josh asked me to cool my jets while he made a few phone calls, I did, but I knew there was nothing he could do. It was only a matter of time before he came to terms with reality like I had, but after all we'd been through together, I felt like I owed him a chance. Trying my best to remain patient, I sat in my cell, rotting.

That afternoon, Josh returned to tell me he'd managed to reach Owen's cousin in the FBI. The man, Agent Ryder *something*, was a stranger to me, but he'd been to college with Josh, Logan, and Caleb. "He's the most honest guy I've ever met," Josh told me. I told him that if he trusted Ryder, I would too. It wasn't really like I had a choice, anyhow.

Josh stayed with me all that evening until a deputy relieved Logan of his duty and shooed Josh off for the night. Then, alone, I lay sleepless on the metal cot for hours, thinking only of my big bed in the farmhouse, my handsome boyfriend, and my adorable puppy—all of which was a million miles beyond my reach. At some point in the night, I must have cried myself to sleep.

Waking at dawn to the sound of keys in the cell door, I opened my eyes to see Logan standing there. "You look awful," he said, sliding the door open. He held up a paper cup of coffee for me. "Agent West from the FBI is here to see you."

"Is that Ryder?" I whispered.

Logan nodded. "He's waiting for you with your attorney."

"Owen?"

"That's the one." He stepped aside to let me out.

I'd hoped Josh would be back before the FBI agent showed up. I'd also hoped for a shower and a comb, but that didn't turn out either. Exhausted and hopeless, I shuffled across the cell, took the coffee from Logan, and sighed. "Lead the way."

Agent Ryder West was waiting in a small room with a large conference table that held only his briefcase. On a tripod next to him, a video camera was pointed at an empty metal folding chair that I knew was reserved for me. A chill ran through me, suddenly worried this friend of a friend wasn't *my* friend at all.

"Miss Carlisle." The agent stood and held his hand out to me, but I was too paranoid to take it. Without a sign of offense, he gestured toward the empty chair. "Please, have a seat. I'm sure you're eager to be done with this."

With Logan behind me, I maneuvered around the table and lowered myself onto the chair. My rear end hurt. If I ever got out of that mess, I promised myself I'd never look at another unupholstered chair again.

Bang!

The crash of metal chair legs hitting the linoleum next to me made me jump. I turned to see a familiar face with messy brown hair settle into the seat he'd just dropped down next to me.

Owen pulled the chair up to the table and smiled at the agent and me. "Ryder, Paige, good to see you both again."

"How's the election coming along?" Ryder asked, smiling back.

Owen shrugged his big shoulders. "Whether I like it or not, I guess." They both laughed as I sat and waited for someone to explain to me what was going to happen to the rest of my life. "Ryder West, let me introduce Paige Carlisle. Paige Carlisle, this is Ryder West."

I nodded my hello, but the tall man came to his feet and held his hand out to me again. Again, I wasn't sure if I should shake it. *What if it's a trap?*

Like a mind reader, Owen pointed his pencil at Ryder's hand. "You can shake it. We're all on the same side here."

"We are?" That was news to me. I shook his hand and found it warm. When I looked up, his smile was pleasant. Sitting back in my seat, I took a sip of coffee to build my courage. "What happens now?" I asked, my eyes flicking back and forth between them.

"Now," Ryder said, "you tell me what happened in North Dakota."

Owen leaned toward me. "This is the only way, Paige."

I stared at Ryder for a moment, and visions of Josh and our life together flashed before my eyes. If I didn't get out of this, everything we'd ever had would be nothing more than a memory. And memories were so terribly fragile.

I took a deep breath and nodded. Ryder pressed record on the video camera and announced my name, the date and time, everyone present in the room, and the reason for the interview.

Sitting with his pen positioned over a yellow legal pad, he asked, "Miss Carlisle, could you please describe how you came to know Walter King Riley of Williston, North Dakota?"

Then, there in that room, I told the agent the whole story, everything I could remember—my father's decade's old affair, my illegitimate half-sister, my lonely life in Nebraska, the stink inside the Wrong Way Tavern, the trap Melody had set for me, the killings, stealing the truck and driving for days without rest before driving it over a cliff, falling in love with Josh—everything.

I spent six hours in that room with my attorney, Owen, and the agent. In the end, I agreed to testify in North Dakota, and they agreed to let me out of the jail on the condition that I didn't leave Whisper Cove—not for anything.

Logan dropped the larceny charge—Josh had never reported the car stolen in the first place. I could have been angry at Logan for all he'd put me through, but honestly, if he hadn't lied to me, I would never have come in. Just like he'd said, I probably would have been killed trying to outrun the gang, which had tracked me down to Maine and cast its members like a wide net over the whole state. Now, not only was I still alive and safe, I had hope of getting my old life back—not the lonely one in Nebraska or the scary one chasing me from North Dakota—but my real life. I belonged in Whisper Cove just like Josh did, and I wasn't going to let anyone take my future from me again.

"They're all in jail," Logan told me as he signed the paperwork to let me out. "We may not be the most sophisticated state when it comes to law enforcement, but we do have the advantage of recognizing people from away when we see them." He never apologized for bringing me in, and I never thanked him for letting me out.

When he released me, Logan gave me the keys to the Mustang, and the first place I drove was the clinic. It had been two days since I'd showered, and I probably smelled like every poor bastard who'd ever been stuck in that jail cell, but I needed to see him, to tell him I was free. I had to apologize for not listening, for being angry and hostile. I needed to thank him for arranging Owen and Ryder—hell, even Logan.

More than anything, I needed to feel his hands on me, his

lips against mine, to stare into his beautiful blue eyes and beg him for forgiveness.

When I raced into the clinic, he was just shutting the office down for the day. He turned to see me, and the look on his face told me I had nothing to thank or apologize for. That big, handsome face was just happy to see me. He threw his arms around me and squeezed me tight. "Thank God," he said. "I love you so much, Paige."

Clinging to him, I whispered, "I love you too."

He never said a word about my smell.

Nevertheless, the first thing I did when I got home was hop in the shower, bringing Josh along with me. We held each other and swayed under the steaming water as it poured from the showerhead. There was no music, but we danced, anyhow.

"I'll do it," he said softly.

With my head against his chest, listening to the beat of his heart, I melted with the soothing rumble of his voice. "Do what?"

"Go to North Dakota with you. I'll bring another vet in… even one from one of those temp agencies, and I'll go to North Dakota while you testify."

"Josh, you can't. You have responsibilities here—"

He lifted my chin from his chest so I was looking up into his eyes. "I have a responsibility to you. And I'm so sorry I hesitated. I'll never do that again, Paige. I promise." He kissed me deeply and held me so close I felt like a part of him. Then he turned the water off, stepped out of the shower, and handed me a towel. "Come on."

I slipped into my robe and wrapped the towel around my long hair, propping the whole thing up on my head, and followed him into the bedroom. As he stood at the dresser, fishing something out of his underwear drawer, I sat on the edge of the bed and waited. "Hurry!" I laughed. "The suspense is killing me!"

"Close your eyes," he told me. I did. I heard his footsteps coming toward me across the hardwood, and I smiled. Then his hand was on my arm as he lowered one knee to floor. "Open them," he whispered.

When I did, I found him holding a black velvet jewelry box. He grinned and opened it before my eyes. I gasped. Inside the box, a beautiful gold band with a heart-shaped diamond sparkled at me. "Josh…" My throat closed before I could say anything else.

"Paige Elizabeth Carlisle, will you please marry me?"

I wanted to scream *Yes!*, but when I opened my mouth, no sound came out. I choked on joy as tears poured from my eyes.

He watched me fall apart, concern surfacing in the lines on his forehead. "Is that a yes?"

Unable to speak, I covered my mouth and nodded frantically.

"Thank God." He took the ring out of the box and slid it onto my left ring finger. Lifting his gorgeous blue eyes to mine as he held my hands, he said, "With this ring, I thee wed."

My voice stolen by the depths of my emotion, all I could do was throw my arms around him and kiss him with all my heart. Josh dropped the velvet box on the floor, swept me up in his arms, and laid me out on the bed. He climbed on top of me, opened my robe, and showered my lips, neck, and breasts with a million passionate kisses.

For hours, we did nothing but touch, feel, and make love. It felt as though we would never get enough of each other. In the end, it was only our exhaustion that made us stop and lie peacefully together.

"I'm going to hire someone," he told me.

"What?"

"A vet for the clinic."

I lifted my head from his chest. "I told you, you don't have to come to—"

He pressed his finger against my lips. "I have to. Even if you didn't have to testify, I'd still hire someone. I don't have a life, Paige. How can I ask you to share yours with me if I don't have one to share with you in return?"

My heart sang.

Josh

Chewing on the end of my pencil, I stared at the applications crowding my inbox. Who knew a position at a tiny vet clinic in the middle of nowhere would draw so much attention?

The month we'd spent in North Dakota had proven too demanding for the temp vet the agency had sent. Now that I was back, I needed to find someone who would be as devoted to the clinic as I was.

I opened the first application and started reading, but it all made my eyes cross. By the fifth résumé, I couldn't even see straight.

"You ready to go home?" Paige came and stood behind me, her hands on my shoulders, kneading away the tension in my muscles. She'd been kind enough to help out at the clinic while Chloe was still on maternity leave. Thank God. I'd never realized how much paperwork Chloe handled until she left me to handle it all alone.

"Not yet." I sighed, leaning back into the massage. "I really need to pick someone, or a couple of someones to interview. I can't keep putting this off. I need help."

"Why don't you forward them to Chloe? She's gonna have to work with them too, and I know, as much as she loves the baby, she's bored to death on maternity leave. I'm sure she'd love to help. She can pick her top three, and you and I will go home, open a bottle of wine, and do the same. Tomorrow, if any of our choices overlap, we'll call them."

"How do you always know just what to do?" I tilted my head back and she leaned down, her soft hair brushing my shoulders, and planted an upside down kiss on my lips.

"I'm good at people. Who else could have convinced Mrs. Preston to limit Muffy's visits to Friday afternoons, so the other dogs wouldn't stress her out so much?"

"That really was a stroke of genius. No more random drop-in visits. No more lingering for hours. Where have you been all my life?"

Her eyes sparkled and her strokes became more suggestive, venturing inside my shirt and across my pectorals. "Come on, Dr, Dalton. I think someone needs some tender loving care. Let's get you home."

"Absolutely, let me forward these emails, and I am all yours."

"Promises, promises," she said, one hand trailing across my shoulders as she walked back to the office to grab her things. "Hurry up! I'm hungry!"

A smile crossed my face as I sent Chloe the latest batch of applicants. I glanced over my shoulder to make sure Paige wasn't watching, and dashed out a hurried message to Mack.

Mack—
If you and Ma were serious, I'd love to take you up on your offer.
—Josh

Chapter Twenty-One

Paige

More boxes came every day. Between my new job as a counselor at the high school and the hours I still put in helping at the clinic, I hadn't had time to sort through them. They piled up in the living room until Josh made the decision to move them into one of the empty bedrooms. Every evening when we got home, he'd carry the boxes in from the front porch and up the stairs.

"You ever gonna sort through these?"

"Thanks for getting them out of the way, babe!" I ignored his question, suspecting it would be a long time before I felt like sorting through the cardboard time capsules of my old life in Nebraska.

"Yeah, yeah."

Jentil followed me into the kitchen and parked himself in front of the oven. "You're lucky dinner's in the crockpot," I told him. His tail wagged, slapping down against the floor a few times before he settled his chin on his paws.

"Is she being mean to you, puppy?" Josh entered the

kitchen and stopped to give Jentil a scratch behind the ears before he made his way to me.

I laughed. “Hardly. I spoil him rotten whenever he visits.” I looked at the puppy and pouted a little. “I miss being his mommy.”

Josh pulled my arms around him and kissed me. “You're still his mommy. You pulled him from the jaws of death when he was just a baby. Dogs don't forget that kind of stuff.”

I nodded, but I still felt a light sadness. “I guess. I just wish he didn't have to keep going back to Mack and Ma's. I know they love him too, but I want him to stay with us all the time.”

“Okay,” Josh said, dropping his hands from the small of my back to the curve of my ass.

“Okay?” I blinked up at him. “What do you mean, ‘Okay?’”

He nuzzled my neck just below my ear. “I mean okay, he can stay.”

I laughed. “What would Mack and Ma say if we didn't bring him back?”

He kissed his way along the curve of my jaw all the way to my lips. “They'd say he belongs with his mommy.”

“You really think so?”

He kissed my lips. “No. I know so.”

I giggled at his tickly pecks and nibbles. “How do you know?”

“Because I already asked.”

My jaw dropped with a gasp, and I stepped back from him. “Really?!”

He smiled and nodded. “That wasn't the reaction I was going for, but yes—really.”

I stepped around Josh and knelt down before Jentil. He lifted his growing puppy face to mine, and his funny little eyebrows quirked up. “Did you hear that?! You're ours now, Jentil! You get to stay here with us!”

Thud, thud, thud. His tail drummed down on the floor again as his eyes looked from me to Josh and back again.

"Welcome home, Jentil," Josh said. Then he stepped up beside me, held a hand out, and nodded toward the stairs. "Come on, beautiful." He didn't have to tell me twice.

Hand in hand, he led me through the living room and up the stairs to our bedroom where he quickly shut the door behind us before Jentil could sneak in. Pushing me back against the door, he leaned in and kissed me. "The rest of our lives, Paige. You and me."

"And that crazy puppy."

"And whoever else comes along." He slid his finger in the gap between the buttons of my shirt, touching the soft skin beneath the silk, sending bolts of electricity that made me weak in the knees. His warm breath stroked my cheek as his thick arms wrapped around me and lifted me up. My legs wrapped around his waist, and my fingers laced behind his neck. Our mouths came together and never parted as he carried me to the bed.

He lowered himself on the edge of the mattress, and I straddled him. With fingers so nimble they could have belonged to a surgeon, he made his way down the front of my blouse, easily slipping the tiny buttons from their holes. When my shirt fell to the floor, he reached around to my bra clasp and made quick work of that too. Sliding the straps from my shoulders, he pulled the lacy black bra off and let that fall to the floor on top of the blouse.

With his arms around the small of my back, he pulled me closer as I threw my head back and offered my breasts to him. My nipples were so hard they ached for his touch, lips, and tongue. He teased me, though, moving his amazing mouth in circles around my pink areolae, refusing to touch the tips until I begged him.

"Please, Josh!"

"Please what?" he asked, playing coy.

"Please kiss them!"

He laughed as his mouth descended on my tender flesh. Sucking one hard pink tip into his mouth, he caressed my breasts with his hands while his teeth toyed and teased. I cradled his head in my arms as he moved from one breast to the other.

"Oh, God…. yes…" I groaned as I rode him through my panties and his blue jeans. There was a straight line of sensation from my nipple to my core that made me hot and desperate to have him in me again. I placed my mouth by his ear and whispered, "I want you inside me."

Suddenly, he hoisted me up and fell back on the bed with me landing on top of him. Giggling, I sat up and ground myself against his bulging crotch as Josh sat up and unfastened the snaps on my skirt, letting it slip to the bed. Completely nude except for my black lace panties, I felt an urgent need to have him naked too.

With his hips between my legs, I bent over him and slid his t-shirt up over his firm abs. Lowering my lips to his stomach, I drank in his wonderful fragrance—part earth, part animal. My fingers worked the button on his faded blue jeans as I slid down to his thighs. Facing his zipper, I slowly pulled it down, gazing up at him with the sultry green eyes I that knew drove him crazy. All at once, his cock sprang free and stood tall and hard.

Trying to hide a crooked smile, I pulled his prick to my mouth and dragged my soft tongue lazily up the length of his shaft as he moaned. When I reached the tip, I licked all around the rim and let my tongue dance over the head, all the time watching my effect on him.

He growled and groaned. His blue eyes rolled back in his head, and his hips lifted off the bed. "Do it, Paige."

I smiled to myself. "Do what?"

"Please, baby." He reached down as if to grab my hair, but

then folded his arms like a pillow beneath his head and watched me.

"Please what?" I batted my lashes innocently.

"Please suck my cock, Paige."

My little smile grew wide. I opened my mouth and descended on his long, thick prick. At first, I just took his knob, spiraling my tongue in growing and shrinking circles. At the same time, I tightened my lips just under the rim and slowly began a gentle bobbing motion. I loved Josh's cock—so eager and responsive, I always knew it liked what I was doing. Opening my jaw wider, I took more and more of him in until the head touched the back of my throat. Pushing down on him just a little harder, I heard him cry out in pleasure as I tried my best to control the muscles in my throat.

After a few minutes, Josh was on the edge of losing his mind. His hands were in fists at his side, and his eyes bulged with wonder as he watched my every move. Finally, I reached down beneath his tender sack and massaged his tight balls. That's when he lost it.

"Stop!" He gently pushed me back while pulling his cock from my mouth. Then he reached down, grabbed me around the waist, and threw me on my back on the bed. He pulled his pants off and climbed on top of me. His thumbs slipped under the elastic sides of my black underwear, and he pulled them down my thighs, over my calves, and off my feet before tossing them aside. "No panties."

He pressed his naked body against mine, and I threw my arms around him, stroked his back, and felt every curve of every muscle in his thick arms. At the same time, he lifted my legs higher and spread them farther apart. His fingers found my mound already slick and ready for him. Gently, they glided up and down between my lips before he pushed harder and found my hungry clit. The warmth of his touch spread instantly through my body, making my hips rise up from the bed in search of more. "Do it, Josh. Please… take me."

He laughed and kissed me. "You want me in here?" He slid his finger inside my slippery opening and gracefully pushed it in up to his knuckles.

"Yes," I groaned, lifting my head from the mattress so my lips could meet his. "Pleeease… more."

He pulled his finger out of my center and slipped it between his lips. "God, you taste good." Grabbed my ankles and parted my legs like wings. Lining the head of his cock to my entrance, he looked down at me dreamily. "I can deny you nothing."

He leaned forward, and the head of his cock popped inside me. "Oh, God! Yes!" He was barely in and already I could feel him stretching the walls of my chasm. "More!" Suddenly, he looked very far away from me… too far. Wrapping my legs around his waist, I reached out, and he grabbed my hands and pulled me up so I was straddling his lap.

It was a new position for me. Josh was already the biggest man I'd ever been with, but this position put him even deeper inside me. I held onto his shoulders with both hands as he reached around and grabbed my rear end in his strong grasp. He pulled me up quickly, sliding himself almost all the way out, and then he paused before slowly lowering me, impaling me on his cock.

"Ohhhhh…. —Josh!" He felt so good so deep inside me, I lost my senses for a moment. My hands slipped from his sweaty shoulders, and I fell backward. I didn't even realize what had happened until I felt his hands lift from my ass to catch me.

"Come here," he said, pulling me back up to him. He held me tight against his chest, laying kisses on the tops of my breasts, and he began a driving rhythm that blew my mind. The warmth I felt, that we shared, was more than any sex I'd ever had before… even with him. I'd never felt so loved, so in tune with another soul before. The pleasure he gave me wasn't earthly. Something divine was transpiring between us.

"Paige," he called out, "I love you!"

"I love you too," I told him, my voice barely more than a disembodied whisper.

Then, without warning, he eased me down on the bed and nestled himself between my legs with his hands pressing down on the mattress at either side of my head. He plowed into me, hard and slow, and pulled out again. That became his rhythm. Each time, like magic, he hit that spot inside me that made my whole body tremble and melt beneath him. I didn't want to come. I didn't want it to end. I knew the moment I reached my climax, he'd come too. Still, I had to. That incredible wave of hot ecstasy washed over me, and I had no choice but to let it carry us both away.

He joined me in that great release, spilling more of himself deep inside me with every slow thrust, shuddering and groaning before he finally relaxed. Rolling me over on top of him, he cradled me in his arms as our lips met in small, loving kisses. I fell into a beautiful post-orgasmic sleep with his cock still buried inside me.

Josh

"Hey, Josh," Logan strolled into the clinic, a toothpick between his teeth. Jentil yipped a greeting before scrambling on his too-big paws and slipping on the freshly mopped floor as he barreled into Logan's ankles. "This shiny government car just rolled into town. Looks federal to me. You expecting Ryder?" He bent down to give a good scratch to the pup's ears.

"No...." I mentally ran through the last few weeks—all the interviews, paperwork, and court appearances. I couldn't think of anything left hanging. I couldn't even remember exactly when I'd last spoken to Ryder

Riiiing...

The bells on the front door chimed, distracting Jentil and sending him scrambling after a new victim. Ryder stepped in from the cold autumn day and nodded to us both. "Josh. Sheriff."

"Ryder." I nodded back.

Logan pulled the toothpick from his mouth and looked Ryder over. "I thought I smelled something. What are you doing here?"

"Is that anyway to greet an old friend?" Ryder laughed and gave Jentil a firm pat.

"Ignore him." I walked over to greet him with a bear hug and a slap on the back. "Logan's living proof of the dangers of prime-of-life celibacy. It's good to see you! We just didn't expect you to grace us with your presence so soon."

"Well, I wish I could say this was a social call, but I didn't plan another trip to the middle of nowhere for no reason. There have been some… developments." He looked around the lobby. "Where is Paige?"

"Uh…" I glanced at Logan, fear suddenly choking me. "I think she's next door at the high school. Ryder, what's wrong? Did something happen at the trial?" I knew it was dragging out, the Hell Dogs' lawyers flooded the courts with appeals, but the FBI had taken Paige's testimony, and the evidence was so overwhelming against the gang, he'd told us she wouldn't have to appear in court."

"No, no. Nothing's wrong. We just have a loose end we need to tie up, and I think Paige is going to want to be here."

Logan stepped forward. "I'll run over and grab her, Josh. You guys stay here." Logan looked me in the eye, signaling that he would take care of her while I wrapped things up at the clinic.

Ryder waved as Logan set off at a rapid clip, much faster than his usual leisurely stroll. After making sure Logan was gone, Ryder turned back to me, putting his official face on. "Josh, what do you know about Melody Grant?"

"Paige's sister?"

"Yeah."

I rubbed the back of my neck. "Not much. Paige barely knew her. She died the day they met." The day was getting weirder and weirder, and I was really starting to worry that something had gone terribly wrong back in North Dakota.

"Mmmmh," Ryder made a noncommittal sound in the back of his throat, staring out the front window where I spotted Logan and Paige hurrying across the parking lot toward us.

They burst through the door together. "Josh! Ryder! What's wrong?!" Her green eyes were huge, and her face was pale despite the chill.

"Here, everybody," Ryder said, opening the clinic door again. "Let's step out to my car. It'll be easier to show you."

Like ducklings we all followed him in a line out to the black suburban parked in front of the clinic. The lights flashed as the agent in the front seat unlocked the doors allowing Ryder access to the back.

"Paige, why don't you come here?" He waved her over to the back door. The windows were tinted so darkly that none of us had a prayer of seeing inside. Pulling open the back door, he bent down, reached in, and then emerging holding a bundle of pink. Jet black hair framed the toddler's tear-streaked face. Sound asleep, her thumb stuck in her mouth, she couldn't have been more than two. "Meet your niece, Ani… Melody's daughter."

"What?" Paige gasped, her hands flying to her face. Then she reached out for the baby, and I knew she'd never let her go again. "Melody had a daughter? How? When?"

"Best we can figure, the gang took her to keep your sister in line. We found Ani in a trailer on a property we raided a few weeks ago. It took us this long to figure out who she was. I know it's a shock, but you're her only family."

"Oh my God!" She clutched the child to her chest as tears

ran down her cheeks and disappeared into the baby's hair. Paige looked to me. "Melody… she didn't turn on me. She was protecting her baby."

"Yes, we think she was. The Hell Dogs used every trick in the book to keep those girls compliant. Blackmail, fear, abuse. Melody didn't stand a chance." He looked between us.

Paige, holding the baby tight against her chest, came to lean against me, and my arms instinctively wrapped around the two of them.

"She needs a home," Ryder said.

I looked down at the woman and child in my arms and the puppy cavorting at my feet. Paige tilted her head back to look at me. Pressing a soft kiss to her forehead and then atop of Ani's, I looked back at Ryder. "She's already there."

KABOOM!

Two streets over, a loud explosion shook Whisper Cove, sending Logan and Ryder into action. Smoke billowed up, and flames shot into the sky just over the general area of Avery's bar. It seemed our small town wasn't done surprising us.

Chapter Twenty-Two

Paige

I sat wrapped in a fleece blanket on the couch with Jentil at my feet, both of us mesmerized by Josh and Ani playing peek-a-boo with the presents under the tree. He'd drop his head behind the big pink box with her new ride-on ladybug toy inside, and even though she could see his feet, she'd squeal with delight every time Da-da popped his head up and said, "Peek-a-boo!" Then Josh and I would laugh and laugh while Jentil wagged his tail.

Eventually, Ani tired of the game and left Josh lonely on the floor. "Where did you go?" he cried.

She smiled and flashed her big green eyes at him even as she lifted her arms to me, and I picked her up and snuggled her into the warm blanket. Ani yawned as Josh crawled across the floor to us. "Somebody's sleepy," I told him as I kissed the top of her head.

"Well, Santa will be here soon, so it's probably for the best." He gently lifted her little hand to his lips and gave her chubby little fingers a kiss.

"Sankoo," Ani chirped.

Josh smiled and rubbed her fingers. "You're welcome."

Careful of Jentil, I came to my feet, lifting Ani with me. "You ready for bed, sweetie?" She shook her head theatrically, but she couldn't hold back another yawn. Resting her head on my shoulder, she accepted defeat, but still wouldn't let go of Josh's finger. Josh, who'd fallen head over heels in love with the little beauty the minute they met, let her lead him up the stairs like a caboose.

"You were born for this," I said, carrying his little princess in my arms.

"What do you mean?"

"Fatherhood, Christmas, peek-a-boo… it comes naturally to you."

"Motherhood must come naturally to you, then, because I would never have had any of this without you."

I smiled. "It's not too much?" I worried about that a lot. Josh had been a workaholic bachelor when we met. In less than a year, he'd become a fiancé, a father, and the owner of a spastic puppy. I knew he'd had no plans for any of it.

"Too much?" He scooped Ani out of my arms and kissed her warm pink cheeks. "It's perfect."

In Ani's room, which he'd painted a soft lavender upon discovering it was her favorite color, he laid her down in her crib and turned to get a book from her shelf. Before he could, I tapped him on the shoulder. "Look. She's out cold."

We both stared down at Ani, admiring her lovely dark hair, her long lashes, those puffy cheeks, and the way she still moved her lips like she was sucking a bottle in her sleep. Careful not to wake her, I covered her with a fluffy white blanket, and he pulled the side rail up and tested to make sure it was secure. Then he put his arm behind my back and escorted me out to the hallway and into our own bedroom.

"We have to fill the stockings," I told him as he began to kiss me.

"In the morning," Josh said, pulling me toward the bed.

I laughed. "No, now. It's what Santa would do."

He grumbled, but went back downstairs, pulled our four stockings from the mantle, and brought them over to the couch. I went to retrieve the bag of stocking stuffers I'd hid in the study. When I came back out, I found Josh looking down, thumbing the angel I'd knitted into Ani's stocking.

"You okay?"

He looked up with a grin on his face and nodded. "What about a nutcracker. Can you do that?"

"For Grant's stocking?"

"Yeah."

"I think so." I sat down next to him on the couch. "I'll find a pattern."

Josh smiled. He set his hand on my stomach and leaned in close to it. "Your mom has mad talents." Then he lifted his head and kissed me. "I can't wait for next Christmas."

HIDE - Whisper Cove, Book 2 *Sneak Peak*

Heather

I stared out at the endless nothing and dreamed of shoving Linnea into it. All was black, except the boat and the frothy crests of waves that carried it, and I longed for the pleasant silence that would follow the *plunk* of her body hitting the cold water. Somewhere, unknown miles in the dark distance, Tall Pines Island awaited us, and it seemed cruel I had to share that miserable journey with a lunatic.

Grabbing the back of the bench, I pulled myself up on uncertain feet to escape her chatter, not that there was anywhere to escape to. Wherever I went, Linnea would follow. Anyway, there was nowhere to go. The bony woman in green scrubs and a wool coat—the 'attendant' or whatever she was—had already warned us that the open deck was strictly off limits and that if I tried to go back there again, she'd restrain me. "For your own safety," she'd said. "There won't be any accidents on the way to the island."

The moment she'd greeted us back on the pier in Boston, I'd known wherever the boat was ferrying us to, I wasn't in for the rejuvenating retreat my mother had promised. "A place for you to relax and not worry about the tense months ahead," Mom said, but I knew the conveniently timed vacation was more for her benefit than mine. Tall Pines was just a place for powerful people to hide black sheep like me… like Linnea.

At the pier, Sheila (as the captain called her) confirmed my suspicions, extending her open palm with a thin-lipped smiled. "I'll take your cell phone, thank you. They'll interfere with the boat's navigation equipment, and there's no service on the island, anyhow."

I surrendered my phones despite my reservations. What else could I do? We were hundreds of miles from anyone and anywhere we knew. One of my mother's goons had already taken all my money when they put me on the plane back at Dulles. "Your expenses have already been paid," Mike told me before he left me on the small jet with no means of escape.

Nearly 24 exhausting hours later, penniless and completely cut off from the rest of civilization on that cursed ferry, I had no desire to make my situation worse with handcuffs or zip ties or whatever the dowdy bitch was planning to use on me. So I sat there and suffered in silence.

Sheila wisely stood watch from the warm and quiet confines of the enclosed cabin. She kept an eye on us through the glass, and though I didn't dare look directly at her, I caught glimpses of her in my peripheral vision. She stood close to the captain and smiled and laughed whenever he spoke. I even spied his fingers touching the curve of her cheek once as she gazed affectionately into his eyes. Clearly, it was not their first cruise together, and it was obvious that their relationship was more than just professional. Time would have passed more quickly if I'd been able to gossip with Linnea about our captors, but subtle conversation wasn't her forte.

There in the dark, I'd had just about enough of her restless babble and insatiable hunger for attention. I had already filled my lungs to finally tell her she could shut her mouth or I'd throw her overboard when the romance at the helm took an unexpected turn. A rise in the woman's volume caught my attention, and I turned my head just in time to see the captain shoving her away from the controls.

Forgetting the warning to remain seated, I came to my feet for a better view. The captain shoved Sheila to the floor, but she climbed to her feet just as quickly as he'd put her down. She rushed toward the control panel and grabbed the radio. This time, when the captain pushed her away, she took the radio with her, ripping it from its mount.

She stumbled backward onto the deck, the radio trailing bits of frayed wires. Standing next to the rail, she glared at him. "You bastard."

"You're a crazy bitch!" He took a step toward her, and she thrust her arm out over the boat rail, dangling the radio wires and receiver over the crashing waves.

"Stop that!" she screamed as moonlight reflected in the trails of tears on her red cheeks. "Stop saying that! I'm not crazy!"

"Shiela, you crazy bi-"

Before he could even finish those words, she turned toward the churning ocean below. The radio slipped through her open fingers and disappeared into the sea.

For a moment, no one said anything. She turned back to the captain, wide-eyed horror plastered to her face. "I…". She looked back over her shoulder at the black water, and then turned her terrified stare back to him. "I…"

A sudden burst of rage took the captain, and he charged toward her. His hands flew up and crashed against her shoulders with all his weight. Her top half fell back over the short rail, her feet left the deck, and we watched in dumbstruck disbelief as she toppled down into the crashing waves below.

For a moment, the captain did nothing but stare down at

the water's endless motion. He seemed as shocked by what he'd done as Linnea and I were. He didn't call her name or reach out to her. The life preserver stayed mounted just a few feet to his side. No valiant effort was wasted on her rescue. Instead, his chest heaved, and he paced back and forth on the deck, muttering to himself.

Linnea came to her feet and took my hand. I was too stunned to rip it away from her. "Oh my God!" she yelled. "You have to save her!"

The captain whipped his head around like he'd forgotten we were there. He looked the two of us up and down and must have realized we were witnesses to the murder he'd just committed.

Taking my eyes off him for only a moment, I glanced left and right in search of a weapon or an escape. There was nothing but the infinite blackness.

All at once, the captain stopped pacing. He took one last look at Linnea and me before he turned his back to us. Like a soldier, he stood at the rail with this arms stiff at his sides and leaned forward. His feet lifted from the deck as his top half teetered over the bannister, and with a splash entirely indistinguishable from the sound of a million rolling waves, he fell face-first into the water below.

Owen

My feet set a steady rhythm in time with my heart, my footfalls hushed by the leaves and duff coating the forest floor. I could feel the heat of the morning roll in as the sun rose, burning away the fog over the ocean. I glanced at my running watch, noting I had just passed the two-mile mark and my heart rate was right where it needed to be. I ran the same route every morning, out the backdoor, through the yard, and into the woods. The five mile loop led me down past the Tuttle house to the beach, across the sand, and then back through town, ending in front of the diner.

I broke through the tree line, jogged a few miles down Driftwood Lane, and through the gate of the white picket fence surrounding the only house for miles along this deserted stretch of rocky Maine coast. I bounded up the front steps and grabbed the letters and junk mail sticking up out of the mailbox. I knocked on the front door, admiring the intricate stone work covered in bright green ivy and the round turrets that made the Tuttle house look more like a castle. *I wonder what kind of furniture fits in a round room?*

"It's open!" Her creaky, aged voice wafted through the open windows. I took hold of the thick brass handle and pushed the heavy wood door open.

"Hi, Mrs. Tuttle. It's Owen!"

"In the kitchen, dear." I followed her voice through the dusty rooms full of solid furniture from a bygone era, most of which was covered in sheets. Mrs. Tuttle kept to the kitchen, the living room, and her bedroom. She said rattling around in the big old house was too much work for her.

"I brought you your mail." I walked into the sunny yellow kitchen where white lace curtains fluttered around the giant bay window looking out over the beach.

"Look at them." She pointed across the sand to the low tide line where the Waterhouse family was bent over, working their way across the beach. Dressed in ratty jeans and thigh-high waders, they used their hand rakes with the long, curved metal teeth to turn sand over and expose the valuable worms underneath. "Can you believe it? How goddamned stupid can you be?"

I shook my head. "They're gonna get fined if Logan catches them."

"And they'll deserve it."

"I'll go talk to them in a minute. They may not know about the new ordinance."

"Hmmmph… high time one of those idiots learned to read." She sniffed, turning away from the window and the worm diggers on the beach, and looked me up and down. "You look thirsty. Want some water? Coffee?"

Still panting, I shook my head. "I really need to keep going. I'm supposed to meet with the campaign planners this afternoon. I've got some paperwork to do before then." I gazed around the bright kitchen that, like Mrs. Tuttle, appeared frozen in time. The wallpaper was the same orange and red flowers I'd known all my life. The yellow refrigerator had been humming in the corner for as long as I could remember. The hand embroidered dish towels she'd probably made herself as part of her wedding trousseau. The whole place was a time capsule Mrs. Tuttle refused to leave.

"You're always in a hurry, Owen," she grumbled.

"I know. I'm sorry. Do you have your tax check for the house and the quarry? I'll drop it off at city hall on my way through town."

"I do. You're such a sweet boy to do this for me." She shuffled to her purse on the table, pulled out her checkbook, and tore the check out slowly. "It's hard getting old. You never remember half of what you should, and what you do remember, no one cares about unless you're giving them money." She made her way to the counter and opened the drawer beneath it. "Here, I'll put it in a plastic bag, so you don't get it all sweaty."

I smiled at her, bustling around in her flowery house dress. "You know I love your stories. I just don't have time this morning."

"I know. I know."

I stood there watching the family on the beach. No one digs worms for fun. The Waterhouses were just trying to survive. Digging worms is back breaking work with no guarantee you'll get paid enough to eat. I'd stopped trying to explain that to Mrs. Tuttle, but I made sure to remind myself whenever I saw them.

"Here you go." She handed me the check all taped up and sealed in plastic. I stuck it in the back pocket of my shorts, snapping it in so I wouldn't lose it.

"Thank you. I'd better head out." I kissed her cheek, and she hummed in happiness, the smile lines around her eyes tightening as she grinned.

"I'll see you tomorrow, Owen, and this time you'll stay for coffee."

I chuckled. "I promise. You stay out of trouble."

"Shoo," she swatted a towel at me, and I jogged out the door laughing.

I ran another few hundred yards along the dirt road to the beach and then made my way across the sand, avoiding the pits and holes left by the diggers. The crisp air, blue waves, and turning leaves were so beautiful, you could almost forget about Whisper Cove's exploding digger population and the joblessness that fueled it. Lack of opportunity had crippled our town since the quarry shut down, and the problem wasn't getting any better.

"Hey guys," I came to a panting halt next to the elder Waterhouses. "You know, the town passed an ordinance banning commercial use of the beach within town limits last month. I just wanted to let you know in case you hadn't heard."

"The old bitch call you?" Keith Waterhouse straightened up from his crouch as far his aching back would let him and spat on the sand at my feet.

"Excuse me?" His venom was nothing new to me, but pretending not to understand was the only civilized response.

"Bitch thinks she owns the beach."

I sighed, wanting nothing more than to continue my run. "Well, technically, she does."

"What the hell does it matter to her? She ain't usin' the worms. Bitch lives in a fancy house, everything she wants at her fingertips. She wants us off the beach, she can come down and throw us off. The Tuttles ain't been shit around here in a hundred years." He squinted at me and scowled. "Or is that what she sent you down to do, handsome?"

"No, that's not my job. I just wanted to let you know." I backed away from the man brandishing the thick tine worm rake at my face. He stood down as I backed away, finally ignoring me and turning back to his digging.

It was hard to feel sympathy for a guy shouting and waving a deadly object in your face. I shivered as I continued my run and thought of the violence that could have unfolded. Mrs. Tuttle was 80 years old, alone in an old house with no way to defend herself if Waterhouse decided to bring the fight to her. I ran harder, desperate to work the unsettling vision out of my head. Sprinting the half mile left on the beach, I was glad to veer from the sand and turn back toward town.

As I pushed on to the last leg of my route, a flash of light out on the rocks and the breakwater caught my eye. My legs stopped, and I shaded my eyes with my hands. The sun was at the perfect spot on the horizon, sitting directly behind the breakwater, making it tough to see the ferry boat stuck out on the rocks. The incoming tide crashed against the vessel, ramming it into the rocks with every wave. There was no way the small craft would come off those rocks in one piece.

"Holy shit." before I could react I spotted the lifeboat drop over the side, and moments later, the ferry was engulfed in flames. The hiss and crackle of the growing fire drowned out the creaking of the boat bashing against the rocks.

The fire grew brighter, almost outshining the sun rising behind it. I watched the tower burn, breaking off and falling into the water with a splash.

Then with a mighty roar, the flames rose higher, the fire breached the engine room, and before I knew it, a heat wave washed over me, and the concussion threw me back a step as the boat exploded.

Download Book 2 to read more!
Driftwood Lane: Whisper Cove, Book 2

Others in the series

Whisper Cove - Allison LaFleur & Beneva Clark

Run: Whisper Cove, Book 1

Hide: Whisper Cove, Book 2

Burn: Whisper Cove, Book 3

Fight: Whisper Cove, Book 4

Sarasota- Beneva Clark

The Darker Side of Mercy

Bachelors Incorporated- Allison LaFleur

Mason: Bachelors Incorporated, Book 1

Damon: Bachelors Incorporated, Book 2

Liam: Bachelors Incorporated, Book 3

Noah: Bachelors Incorporated, Book 4

Ryder: Bachelors Incorporated, Book 5

Luke: Bachelors Incorporated, Book 6

Jace: Bachelors Incorporated, A Novella

Wilder: Bachelors Incorporated, A Christmas Story

About Allison LaFleur

I can't imagine a better life than traveling and spinning my stories across all seven continents. You might just spot me one day with my iPad on my tray table at 32,000 feet typing the hours away!

I call the Florida Keys home with my family and two tea cup yorkies. After work I like to unwind by watching the sun set over the ocean, reading and writing on the porch.

Want to connect with me? Great! I love to hear from my readers. You can find me Facebook, GoodReads, and Amazon, or simply send an email to:

allison@allisonlafleur.com.

About Beneva Clark

Beneva Clark started life in Portland, Maine but spent most of her childhood and teen years around Augusta, which is roughly an hour north but feels like a distant and far less sophisticated planet.

After years of catechism, high school football games, and more alone time than is healthy for a developing human, her writing was published by a local newspaper.

Clark first attempted fiction over the summer between her junior and senior year of high school. It was terrible. Two decades passed before the chance to try again presented itself.

Beneva Clark currently lives on the Gulf Coast of Florida with her son and is deeply grateful for the opportunity to build worlds, create characters, craft stories, and share them with you.

http://www.benevaclark.com

www.ingramcontent.com/pod-product-compliance
Lightning Source LLC
Chambersburg PA
CBHW030520310726
48979CB00010B/1743/J

* 9 7 8 1 9 4 8 6 5 7 4 0 2 *